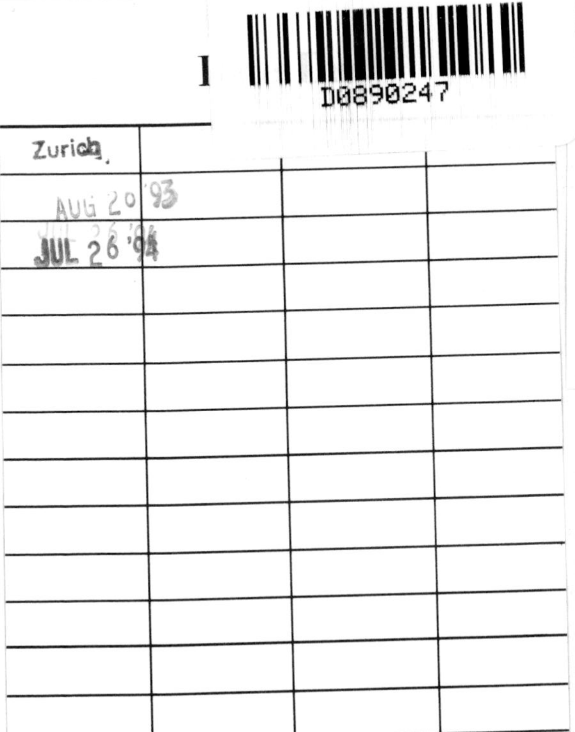
D0890247
HURON COUNTY LIBRARY
Zurich
AUG 20 '93
JUL 26 '94

BURNING ISSY

MELVIN BURGESS

BURNING ISSY

Andersen Press · London

For Donkey

With acknowledgements to Jim Walker

First published in 1992 by
Andersen Press Limited,
20 Vauxhall Bridge Road, London SW1

British Library Cataloguing in Publication Data
Burgess, Melvin
Burning Issy
I. Title.
823'.914[J]
ISBN 0–86264–381–3

Typesetting by Tek Art Limited, Croydon, Surrey
Printed and bound in Great Britain by Courier International Limited, East Kilbride

Cover illustration by Linda Hennessy

Preface

The Christian God is the God of love, the Bible teaches us. But the Church has not always remembered. In 1613 eight people were hanged at Lancaster, just a few of the hundreds of thousands who died for the same reason all over Europe. They had been found guilty of witchcraft. Now we live in more enlightened times, but the killer's vision remains in our eyes. A witch is still a figure of evil, even though the name of their persecution – Witch Hunt – is the name we give to every fanatical attempt to destroy the harmless.

Many of those killed were simply old, or ugly or poor or victims of religious bigotry and frightened neighbours. But the idea remains that some really were witches – not old ladies in tall black hats, but the survivors of an old religion that worshipped nature. What might these people have been like?

They were not rich or powerful, they did not read or write and they have left us no record whatsoever. Misrepresented, misunderstood, abused and at last totally destroyed, nothing is known of them but what their enemies have told us. This is a story for them. It is not a story about good and evil, or an attempt to show things as they really were, because that would deny the world as they saw it and believed it. I have tried to show how it may have felt to live then . . . to believe that God was jealous and cruel, that the fires of hell awaited sinners like yourself, that the Devil walked the earth and that witches had evil powers and were near . . . in your village, in your family . . . maybe even inside yourself.

Chapter 1

There was a lot of talk about God but it was the Devil we really feared. Witches lived in the villages and farms. On nights when they gathered to worship, the Devil came up from hell and walked among us, in our fields, on our moors. In the street you might brush against a man who had kissed him not a few hours back. Once, some boys showed me a mark on Pendle Hill where they said the Devil had walked. It was the print of a cloven foot like a cow's only bigger. A few metres further on were the remains of a fire. The boys asked me what the Devil looked like and where he had kissed me. When I said he never had they didn't believe it.

'Burning Issy,' one of them jeered. That was my nick-name. But they didn't dare touch me.

It took so little. Just an accusation from a spiteful neighbour and you could be arrested. If you were arrested you would be tortured and if you were tortured you would confess and be hanged. Innocent cottagers who would have run a mile at the whiff of witchcraft had been executed just for knowing how to treat a cold. I was a mystery. I was brought out of the North when I was only two years old with nothing but my name and a dream of fire. No one expected me to live, but I did.

That's the way I mean to keep it.

When my foster-father set out that morning there was a hard frost and the donkey's hooves clattered on the frozen earth. By the time he reached Colne the wind was flinging icy rain across the streets and the ground underfoot had begun to melt and turn the tracks slippery. Nat was regretting that he had chosen such a foul day to fetch his supplies. He was walking past the market stalls by the donkey's side when he saw a woman running through the puddles towards him carrying a bundle of filthy, half-burnt rags in her arms. She was wearing nothing but a smock and a shawl, her feet were bare and she was wet through. He could tell by her wobbling run that she was at the end of her strength. That was not unusual. But what was striking about her, he said, was the way she carried that bundle of rags – not like a beggar woman with an armful of rubbish, but as if she bore a treasure over the muddy streets.

She ran up and thrust the bundle at him. Nat opened the blankets and saw – me. The strangest, ugliest little face looked back at him, a mess of patches of bright red skin and fat yellow lumps. It wasn't just the blanket that had been burned. I was scorched scarlet and covered from head to foot in great yellow blisters.

'I've no means to bring her up,' said the woman, in a Scots accent. 'Her mother's murdered and I'm driven out of my home.'

Nat never thought but picked me up and put me on the donkey. He took out a loaf of bread and gave it to the woman, who nodded. They walked on a few steps but then turned back to look at one another and they both laughed because it looked as if Nat had swapped the baby for the bread. Nat remembered her laugh in particular, he said, because it was such a happy, gurgling, delighted noise, despite all her obvious misery.

As he looked through the rain at her he saw that she too had burnt skin on her hands and face, long blisters reaching over her cheeks. Her hands were wrapped in bloody rags.

'She's called Isabel,' the woman called across to him, past the people hurrying in between them, past the rain and the wind. 'She's two years old.' Nat nodded again, the woman smiled and ran off, splashing and stumbling through the holes in the road to take shelter under some awnings in the market. She chewed her bread and watched as he led the donkey up the road until they were hidden from each other by the market day crowd.

I was wrapped in a dirty woollen shawl that was just a web of tatters and wear. My new foster-father threw it away within the first ten minutes and bought me a little woollen blanket to keep me warm on that cold December day. It was a sign that the woman knew something about people that the first thing Nat thought of was to spend his money on keeping me warm.

Nat was not a young man. His wife had died

three years before, he lived alone with his daughter Kate and his son Ghyll and he could not afford another mouth to feed. But he spent the money anyway and had to go without the tools he wanted to buy. I was blue with cold, half-starved and too weak even to cry. I coughed like a cat in that blanket all the way home and when we got there Kate told him he was an idiot to spend the money, anyone could see the baby would be dead within a week. But here I am still, thanks to Nat's big heart.

'I'd rather have the loaf of bread,' said Ghyll, whenever Nat told the tale. It had become part of the family history and I could never hear it often enough, as if I might get some clue to myself from the re-telling.

As for the woman, she disappeared. Nat believed she'd died and blamed himself for not bringing her back home with the baby. There were rumours of a Scots woman settling near Hebden Bridge and marrying into the cloth trade, but whether it was her or another we didn't know. She never got in touch.

Kate underestimated her father. Nat had the gift of healing. My pitiful red and yellow face soon mended, and as I grew older the scars faded, until in the end all that was left was some shiny skin around my cheeks and eyes where the burns had been deepest. Isabel got shortened to Issy, and I became part of the family.

The memory of my burning was slower to heal. Even a candle by my bedside frightened me at first and Nat had to keep me behind a screen where I couldn't see the fire on the hearth. I woke up screaming every night for weeks, and although the dream became less frequent with time, it never left me. Even today when I stand too close to a blaze, my heart begins to race and my scars itch and throb and I remember how it was . . .

. . . Without warning, violently, I'm snatched up into a blinding, searing light. My face is scorched, flames beat the air before me, around me. I'm trying to turn my head, but it's frozen, I'm trying to scream but the heat sears my throat, I'm gagging on the hot air, screwing up my eyes, thrashing, twisting, but there's no escape . . . And then I open my eyes . . .

There was a face, there was always a face. And that face terrified me. I saw it clearly in the dream, but after waking I could never remember it. It was right in the fire, burning. The fire was getting hotter and closer and at last I managed to snatch a lungful of hot air and scream something – a word, I never knew what – so loud I woke myself up.

Nat told me I must have had an accident when I was small. Others had different ideas. There were those who said that a girl who came from nowhere had something to hide and that my dream was a memory of the place I came from. As for the face

– that was the face of him who owned me: the Devil in hell. They were the ones who called me Burning Issy. Heaven help me, I used to believe them, but I know better now.

Our parson, Parson Holden, didn't agree that I came from hell. But he thought hell was where I was heading and that the dream was a warning to me to stay in the ways of God. The parson was not a bad man and considered it a special duty to help me. I did not understand why God should have singled me out in this way, but I was very sure about one thing: whether the fire was from my past or in my future, I above all things wanted never to come near it. Every night I prayed for God to keep me safe. I would have done anything to keep the face from me.

Chapter 2

We were poor, but there were a great many poorer than us. We rented a cottage and a small plot of land a few miles under Pendle Hill where we kept pigs and chickens and grew vegetables. Sometimes Nat helped with the harvest or did a little manual work, but he wasn't a clever man with his hands. Mostly, he was a cunning man. He could cure a sick cow or a pig or help someone to get well just by sitting with them and he knew all the curing herbs in the fields and the woods. People came from miles around to get his help, and when they were too ill, he went to them. He always went, whether they could pay him or not. Most of his patients were poor; he made a small living with his gifts. It was not a safe profession, either. In those days even good Nat's friendly charms were suspect. Miller Bawdwin, the church warden, claimed they were the Devil's work and complained to the magistrate, Roger Nowell, and even further afield to get Nat arrested. Parson Holden warned Nat to give up his work, but Nat said that his gifts came from God, and that God would not allow him to suffer for practising them.

Ghyll, being Nat's son, had the gift too. When I was five years old he bought some warts on my hands off me. He paid me a fat blackberry for each one and the next morning my palm began to clear up. When he was grown up, he would be a cunning man in Nat's place.

Ghyll was not always a good friend. He was four years older than me, he was a boy, he had the gift of a cunning man and he thought that I was beneath him. We lived away from the village and people avoided us because we were a cunning man's children. The word of my fire dream did not help, or my nick-name. When Kate was fifteen she married and went to live with her husband in Burnley, and I took over her duties – the cooking, the cleaning, the household chores. I was eight years old.

When I did have time I often used to go off to play by myself. One favourite place was a wooded nook by a little stream about a mile from our house. When I was small I used to go there to play with my doll, which Ghyll had carved for me out of a piece of wood for my seventh birthday. Later on it was a good place just to go and be on my own by the stream where no one ever came.

That was where I first met Jennet.

I was scared at first. I had seen her before many times, begging with her mother or grandmother. She was the same age as me, twelve, but so much smaller with years of poor food and cold that she might have been two or three years younger. I knew what she was and where she came from. My first thought was to run, but I was not going to give up my favourite place so easily.

'What are you doing here?' I demanded.

Jennet only shrugged and moved a little towards something down on the damp moss close by the stream. It was some twisted, ugly thing that might have been the figure of a person. I looked fearfully at it and thought of witchcraft.

'What is it, what are you doing?' I hissed.

'It's my doll,' whined Jennet. She looked sulky. 'I'm only playing,' she added.

'This is my place,' I began angrily. But even as I spoke I saw what was going on. The doll was just a forked stick with some horse hair stuck on one end, and it was the only toy she had. She had laid it where I used to play with my doll. She must have hidden and seen me playing here and come after with her poor old stick, and that was as near as she got to someone to play with. Being what she was, Jennet must be even lonelier than I.

'How did you know about this place?' I asked.

'I saw you,' she admitted, looking up at me to see my reaction. But I wasn't scared of her any more, or angry. I was curious, and I was wondering already if it was possible to be friends with someone like her.

Jennet was a witch's child. All her family were known for it. She was not one of them, not yet. I'd been afraid of her kind all my life but now I only felt sorry for her – she was so poor and hungry and frightened, and had nothing to look forward to, not even her reward in heaven, since she would have to sell her soul to the Devil when she was old enough. Jennet was bad luck to everyone, even to her own family in the end. But she was good and loyal to me, then and later on, and I never regretted being her friend.

Chapter 3

Jennet lived in Malkin Tower, an old, half blown-down wooden building a few miles up from us towards Pendle Hill. Her grandmother was Old Demdyke, the worst witch of them all. She often passed our house on her way to beg in Colne and she always stopped to ask for something. Jennet's mother was a terrible-looking woman called Squinting Lizzie because of the way her two eyes stuck out of her head, one up, one down.

Lizzie had a vicious temper but it was Old Demdyke we feared the most. She was as blind as the night and so full of spite and misery it just spilled out of her, like an old crock too full of water. She had been a witch for over fifty years and everyone had a tale to tell of how she had cursed the animals, or turned the milk or beer sour. Over the years she had murdered maybe a dozen poor souls with her witchcraft, sometimes for no more than refusing her a crust of bread. That's what people said, at least. But I'll say this, that the Devil never took care of his creatures. Demdyke had a long life but every day of it was spent in want.

Nat always gave them something, not from fear but because he pitied them. He said that the tools of beggars had always been pity, disgust and fear, and that talk of curses was just to help folk part with their money. He never believed they could do what people claimed. Nearly everyone felt obliged to refuse the witches from time to time when they came begging, just to show whose side they were on, and if Nat had pitied less and thought more of his own skin he would have turned them away once or twice a year himself.

Jennet was a dangerous friend to have – dangerous for me and for Nat. I told myself that she was not a witch, not yet, and hoped for the best. She was my first friend. I'd spent my whole life doing the right thing – surely to have just one friend couldn't be all that bad, even if that friend was Old Demdyke's grand-daughter. Poor Jennet, she wasn't much, but I loved her.

Between hunger, cold and exhaustion, Jennet was always suffering in some way. I stole pieces of bread and left-overs for her, which she gobbled up like a hungry little dog. Once I found her an old vest that was too small for me. When she took off her smock to put it on, I realised with a shock that the smock was all she had against the frosty wind. She had pasty blue flesh, marked with black bruises and scars and scabs and you could count her little ribs sticking out. She saw me looking and covered herself up quickly. But it was a waste of time giving her clothes. The vest was gone the very next day, stolen by her sister Alizen, even though she'd had to rip it up to get it over her big head.

We had both spent so much time on our own that neither of us really knew how to play together, but we did our best. I brought my doll along. It was a crude thing, but it had eyes, a nose and a face as well as arms and legs, unlike Jennet's piece of stick. When she was allowed to hold this wonderful plaything, Jennet was overjoyed, and when I told her to do something, such as to put the baby to bed, or to give her a drink, she always did it as if I had just had the cleverest idea in the whole world. Although we were the same age she was so much smaller and simpler that I thought of her as a little sister.

The thing Jennet loved best was listening to tales about home. She couldn't hear enough of what Ghyll and Nat and I said and did, what we ate, even what we fed to the pigs or the chickens, or how we did the housework, as if our poor little cottage were heaven on earth. In exchange for these tales, she offered to whisper curses and charms to me. I remembered what the priest had said and shook my head. I told her about my dream.

'I'm not going to that fire, not if I can help it,' I told her.

Jennet looked forward to becoming a witch because she thought the others would stop being cruel to her, but she was miserable that she had to go to burn in hell rather than go to heaven with the Christian folk. 'It would be nice to have someone friendly down there with me,' she told me wistfully. She offered to ask Demdyke about my dream. She was in awe of Demdyke, who seemed to know everything. But I told her not to.

I added her to my prayers after that. Neither of us wanted to go to hell and burn forever. But it seemed that between Old Demdyke and my dreams, we were both heading that way.

It was about then that Ghyll began to ask questions.

Ghyll was fascinated by any kind of magic. He was always trying out brews and charms. When the witches came begging and Nat was out, Ghyll offered them a piece of bread in return for a charm and they always gave him one. He pestered them for more, and Old Demdyke told him to meet her at Malkin Tower and she'd show him. But although he was bold enough at home, he didn't dare go there.

Ghyll was a fool to himself. For one thing, no one would use him as their cunning man if he got a name as a witch. For another, he was putting all of us in danger. Nat begged him and beat him for it, but never enough to make him stop.

I put up a show of not wanting to tell him. Jennet had asked me not to tell anyone about us, but he was a big brother to me and I wanted to impress him even though I knew it was a stupid thing to do.

The next time I went across the moor to meet Jennet, Ghyll came with me. I can remember now how she looked when I appeared over the lip of the little valley above the stream – her thin white face and her big black eyes looking over my shoulder at Ghyll coming down after me. No sooner had I made a friend than I betrayed her. I knew it would never be the same again between us.

'Witch's child,' said Ghyll. 'Tell me some spells.'

Jennet whispered her charms fearfully, as if she were reciting the most awful secrets. But Ghyll was disappointed. He scoffed that every baby knew these silly old rhymes, and he thought that Jennet was trying to make a fool of him. He was sulky about it, but I noticed he wasn't bold enough to bully her. Instead, he begged her to take him and hide him near her house next time there was magic being made. Jennet found it hard to believe that anyone would want to go near such secrets, but Ghyll insisted. She looked at me. I shrugged.

'Why not, if he wants to,' I said.

The truth was, despite my fear, despite Parson Holden, despite hell-fire . . I was curious, too.

Chapter 4

The first time Jennet came to fetch us Nat was in and we couldn't get away. She came again at twilight when he was out to see a sick child. I said I'd come, too, and she threw me a pained, wistful look. I knew she'd rather I stayed behind, but I wasn't backing out, not now. I'd been called a Devil's child so many times, I wanted to see what people thought I was. We ran inside for our capes and hoods and followed her up the hill.

Malkin Tower stood in the corner of a muddy pasture on the ridge of a hill. Behind was the greater hulk of Pendle Hill but in the other direction was a clear view across Colne and Marsden, and to the north-east to Earby and beyond, right up into the Yorkshire Dales. Once, it had been used as a look-out tower, but the years of wind and wet had taken off the cladding at the sides and even the timbers beneath. Now a couple of great rotting beams pointed miserably to heaven above a green mound crouched low on the ground where the witches had bent branches and heaped up turfs as a roof. There were no windows, but they had an old wooden door, patched and rotted and ill-fitting though it was. All around, at this time of year, was a shallow bog of trodden mud and water that flowed in towards them, and they had built a low wall of earth and stones to keep the water from coming right into the earth floor of the hovel itself.

Before long we could see flames flickering ahead. The witches had built a fire in the field outside their home. In half an hour we were near enough to see them, sitting crouched under the broken beams, at some kind of work in the firelight. Jennet led us round to one side behind a low dry-stone wall and told us to be quiet.

There was a gusty, cold wind flicking rain at us from all directions and beating the flames into angry shapes. The fire roared and heaved and threw flights of sparks far across the fields. I could feel my hands sweating. I thought I'd seen that fire before. I began to pant with fear.

'It's just to keep warm – it's a cold night,' whispered Jennet. She touched my cheek briefly and whispered, 'Go, quickly.' But I shook my head. I couldn't have moved if I'd wanted to. Jennet slipped away to join her family. I couldn't stop shaking.

'Ssssh!' hissed Ghyll. I realised I was gasping aloud. He pushed me down into the dirt and I lay there hugging the mud, listening to the roar of the fire and trying to calm myself.

The fire had been recently stoked up with fresh wood, but it soon settled down to a steady glow. I began to feel better and peeped through a crack in the wall to see what they were doing.

Old Demdyke was sitting on a stone in the mud as close to the fire as she could. She was covered from head to foot in rags, wrapped round and over her head so that only her bony face showed. Her daughter, Squinting Lizzie, sat to one side of her, also wrapped up like a parcel in rags and by her side was Jennet's elder sister, Alizen. Demdyke's son, James, sat behind with Jennet, his chin in his hands, watching them.

Demdyke, Lizzie and Alizen held something on the ground with their hands which they were pressing and moulding. As they worked, they spoke quietly to themselves. They never looked up or stopped their mumbled chant and they were so still and composed that I might have thought that here were people at prayer, had I not known better.

Apart from the kneading action between their knees, the only one to move was Squinting Lizzie. Since her eyes were set so crookedly in her head she had a habit when she looked closely at something of turning her head to see first from one eye, then the other . . . then, from one, then the other. Now her head moved regularly from side to side . . . tic, toc . . . tic, toc . . . like a fierce, quick bird.

Lizzie lifted her work up to see it better by light. She was moulding a small figure. She turned it to and fro, shook her head from side to side, and scratched at its face with her nail. She sighed, pulled her wraps closer and inched nearer the fire, as if she could somehow wriggle right into the embers without getting scorched.

Demdyke stared straight ahead into the fire, warming her blind face and keeping her work out of sight. Her lips moved ceaselessly and it was clear that nothing existed in her world but the making of that small figure. Alizen, on the contrary, seemed to be having difficulties. Jennet had told me that Alizen had been a witch for only a few years and was no good at it at all. She frowned and sighed as she laboured heavily on her little model. Her mother Lizzie kept turning to glare at her.

'Well, how's your work?' she asked at last, turning her face to the fire so that she could see Alizen sitting by her shoulder.

'Good enough,' replied the girl cautiously.

'You'll find out in a week or so,' muttered her mother.

'If you put your soul into the work the Devil will know and do as you ask,' said Demdyke suddenly, lifting up her face as she spoke, so that we could see the blank hollows of her eyes. 'A witch works with her soul, not her fingers. If my hands were cut off, I could still turn a man into his own shadow.'

'Let me see,' demanded Lizzie. She snatched the figure her daughter was working on and held it in the light, scowling. She was not pleased with what she saw. 'Even when she works she produces nothing,' she hissed, and flung the little thing in the girl's face. 'You're not fit to beg,' she screamed. For a second I thought she would strike her and I closed my eyes and hid deeper in the shadow of the wall. But she just squatted back down and spat at the fire.

'Give it to James,' she snapped. 'Those swine at the mill won't go unpunished for your sake.'

Alizen gave her work to James, who came and took her place by the fire while she vanished into the shadows behind, out of harm's way.

'Take some more wax and try for the baby,' ordered Demdyke. Alizen got up and went into the house for more wax. She sat down close to the fire again and began warming it in her hand to make it workable.

'They're calling people's souls to come and live in those figures,' whispered Ghyll excitedly. 'They can harm the body by harming the models. I wish they'd speak louder; I'd give anything to know the verses for the calling of souls.'

'Why should they want to hurt Bawdwin's new baby?' I asked. I'd seen the baby a few days ago when I went with Nat to buy nails. I'd begged to hold it and it had gurgled in my arms and peed down my shoulder, making everyone laugh. Surely a new baby could have done the witches no harm.

Ghyll shrugged. 'Bawdwin wants to see them hanged. I heard Demdyke went there to beg the other day and he whipped her off his land. Now we'll see how well the Devil does her work.'

Ghyll was getting impatient. He could see spells being worked but he couldn't hear them, and I think he would have tried to creep over the wall to get closer. He never had the chance. A few minutes later, Old Demdyke suddenly turned her head. Someone spoke; she hushed them with a hiss and a wave of her hand, put down her work and stood up. Everything went still. I pressed my face into mud. I knew at once she knew where we were. Don't ask me how – I just knew.

'Please, God, keep her away,' I prayed. But I was too fearful to run. I hadn't learned then to trust my instincts and I was frightened of making a noise.

I opened my eyes and peered through the gaps in the wall once more. Demdyke was sniffing and turning her head this way and that like an animal testing the air. She moved in a slow circle, turning, sniffing, turning – until she was directly facing the wall where we hid.

'James, Lizzie,' she called. She gestured to them and they ran each to one side of us and over the wall. As soon as they were in position, Demdyke hobbled straight towards us.

'I smell strangers,' she hissed. She crouched over her stick and moved so fast she might have been on wheels, her blind eyes fixed on us as if she could see us right through the stone wall. As she came, Lizzie and James closed in from either side.

That second Ghyll broke and ran for it, but as soon as he got to his feet he showed up in the firelight and James was on him. I heard the thud and shout as he hit the ground and the squeal of pain as James dragged him to his feet. I tried to slide under the shadow of the wall away from Lizzie, but the witch seemed to know exactly where I was. She pounced on me as if I were a rabbit and dragged me up by my hair. I fought back – I only needed to break her grip and she wouldn't have caught me if she'd had the wind to ride. But her hand flung back and I got a violent blow on my ear that knocked me twisting into the mud. My head was spinning and my ear buzzing as she dragged me up again and kicked me over the wall and into the circle of firelight where Demdyke was waiting.

Chapter 5

'What does our Master order us to do with spies?' demanded Demdyke.

Lizzie gave me a shake and prodded me in the ribs, edging me closer to the flames. 'Burn 'em,' she hissed.

'And what does he promise us for the bodies and souls of Christians?'

'Power and wealth,' replied James on the other side. Ghyll squealed, and I could see that his arm was being forced up his back. His face was white, but Ghyll was no coward and he was not to be put down.

'I'm not frightened of you,' he told the old witch. 'My father can deal with you. He gets called in to undo all your spells. You can't harm me.'

'Is it a challenge?' jeered Demdyke. 'The cunning man against the witch? Do you want to find out?'

Lizzie gave a short, barking laugh. 'My mother can make your father's bones burn the flesh off him,' she snorted. 'And so can I.' All the time, she was edging me into the embers at the edge of the fire. She knew I had a fear of fire. Already I had to hold my face to one side to avoid the heat.

Ghyll just repeated, 'I'm not frightened of you,' in a high voice.

Demdyke laughed. 'This is the boy who knows

so much, he begs hexes off me every time he sees me. I told you to come to Malkin Tower and I'd teach you something, and so I will.' She gestured to Alizen. 'Bring me wax,' she ordered.

Alizen ran off into the hovel and returned with a lump of dirty black wax. She knelt down by the fire to warm it in her hands and make it workable. Meanwhile, Lizzie was still prodding me in the back with her hard, spiteful finger.

'You'll burn, you little rabbit, you'll burn . . .' she kept hissing, pushing me closer and closer to the fire so that my bare feet stumbled on the hot ashes. At last I tripped and if she hadn't hauled me back at the last second, I'd have fallen head first into the red-hot mass.

'Don't push me, I can't stand the fire!' I screamed, and shoved back so violently that strong as she was, Lizzie all but fell and lost her grip.

Demdyke turned to me. 'The girl out of the North,' she said. 'Isabel a-Style.'

'My name's not a-Style,' I replied shakily. 'I'm an orphan. No one knows my real name.'

'Isabel a-Style,' repeated Demdyke. 'I knew your grandmother, and your mother. I know the fire that's waiting for you. If you give my Master your soul, I'll save you.'

I stared at her. She nodded blindly back. But before anymore was said Alizen handed her the warmed wax and she began to model with it. With dirty, deft fingers she quickly formed the shapeless lump into a rough figure. Then, she reached out, wrapped a coil of Ghyll's hair around her finger and tugged it out of his head. Ghyll shouted and jumped, but James held him fast. Demdyke worked the hair into the figure and again reached out her hand. Now she wanted to know his face. Her long fingers moved over him, caressing his cheeks, feeling gently into the sockets of his eyes, around his ears, his nose, his lips.

'Bite her!' I thought. But Ghyll was paralysed. He closed his eyes, stopped breathing. She made herself familiar with every corner of his face.

She took up her model again, pinching and stroking confidently and quickly. When she held it up a few seconds later, it was Ghyll's own face that stared back at him from the witch's hand – a rough image, but it was him.

He made a lunge for it but Demdyke jerked it back and laughed. 'He knows enough to be scared,' she jeered. 'What shall I do with it? Give it to you?' She held it out close to him, but James held him tight and he couldn't move. 'The fire?' she asked. She held the little model near the embers. 'It would easily melt . . .'

'Don't . . .' croaked Ghyll. 'Give it me, I'll do whatever you want.'

Demdyke leered triumphantly. 'Alizen – fetch me Tibb,' she commanded.

Alizen fetched a basket which she laid before the old woman. A quick little snout appeared over the edge of the rush-work, and out snaked a long, sinuous shape. It was like a weasel or a stoat, but larger. Its eyes were entirely white, like Demdyke's; it too was blind. It stood upright like a man and turned its head from side to side, nosing the air in exactly the way Demdyke had done when she was searching us out behind the wall. Then it let out a shrill cry, jumped out of the basket and across the ground to her. It ran up her leg and round to her side, where it seemed to be trying to burrow its way under her clothes.

Even Lizzie seemed cowed by this strange, long creature. I pressed back into her. I was looking at Demdyke's devil.

'This is my imp, Tibb,' said Demdyke softly. 'I gave him my soul and I feed him my blood and he does what harm I wish. Watch.'

She lifted up her shawl and the rags on her side, and exposed a stripe of her tired flesh to us. She was every bit as thin as Jennet, and I thought how horrible it was for her to have lived and starved for so long. On her waist was a dark mark and to this the creature nosed its way. It moved its head quickly, up and down. Demdyke let out a soft cry and the blood flowed. Tibb began to lap it up.

'There, drink, drink and do harm for me, Tibb,' murmured the witch. There was silence except for the hiss and crackle of the fire and Demdyke's regular little breaths. Tibb hung silently off her, only scratching the wound and squeaking impatiently when the flow was too thin.

Demdyke straightened up and pushed him away. The creature squealed angrily and tried to find its way back under her clothes.

'I have other drink for you today, Tibb, dear,' she said. She took him up by the scruff of his neck and showed him to Ghyll. 'Tibb will make a mark on you and drink your blood. Then he will have taken your soul and you will be one of us.'

Ghyll twisted to one side, but James grabbed his jerkin and pulled it up. His chest heaved and the whites of his eyes flashed in the firelight as Demdyke came with the imp. When she got close, Ghyll began to fight with all his strength.

'I won't do it, I won't do it, let me go!' he shrilled, tearing his jerkin desperately down and trying to escape.

To my surprise, Demdyke backed off. 'If you won't join us, then you'll have to buy your mannikin,' she told him. She handed the imp back to Alizen, who quickly put it back in the basket. Demdyke crept up close to Ghyll. 'Tomorrow your father will kill a pig,' she whispered. 'Bring me a bowl of its blood and some of the meat and I'll give you the mannikin back.'

'How do I know you'll give it me?' asked Ghyll.

Demdyke grinned. 'Trust me,' she said.

Ghyll stared at her grinning face and suddenly he spat at her. 'You'll never give it back,' he croaked. 'I'd trust anything before I'd trust a witch like you.'

Demdyke wiped the spittle from her face with a vicious look at Ghyll. 'Then we'll watch you burn,' she screamed. She bent down and moved the mannikin closer and closer to the fire, until the little head began to turn shiny with melting wax.

Sweat was dripping off Ghyll. His breath came in short, rasping gasps. I twisted round to look at him and it seemed to me that I could feel how the heat was burning deeper and deeper into his flesh. Soon I could actually see red marks creeping from his hair down his face, and Ghyll began to moan in pain.

The heat from the fire, the stench of the hovel and the witch close by me, the bruises and pokes and above all the fear affected my mind – I began to feel that it was I who was burning. I was choking and swooning: then the flames came. I could see them all around me, I could feel my throat scorching, my own flesh turning red and black. My nightmare was alive. I tried to scream, tried to turn my head but couldn't. Then I forced open my eyes. There was the face before me, the face I never dared remember . . . I twisted and thrashed my head from side to side . . . I screamed and screamed and screamed . . .

The flames vanished abruptly. I saw Demdyke spinning round on her heels as if she had been violently struck. James and Lizzie ran towards her, but she spun right round and into the fire on her back in a cloud of sparks. Ghyll turned and ran but I was rooted to the spot. James dragged his mother out of the fire by her heels, turned her over in the grass and began beating at the glowing rags on her back. But the witch was so covered in cloth that it did not reach her skin, and in a second she was on her feet again, literally smouldering, clutching her arm and glaring at me.

'Witch yourself!' she screamed. 'You burned me, witch. This arm never touched the flames.' And she pushed up her rags to show the arm that had held the mannikin. The skin was a livid red right up to her hand, as if it had been plunged into fire.

'Grab her!' shouted Demdyke. James and Lizzie took a step towards me, but they hesitated to touch me now, and I was suddenly able to turn and run off down the hill after Ghyll – away from the fire, away from the witches, away from the scene of what I already knew was my crime against man and God.

Chapter 6

When Nat learned where we'd been he was furious. He meant to beat us both, but when he saw how frightened we were he decided we'd learnt our lesson already. He made it clear I wasn't to see Jennet anymore and made Ghyll swear never to have anything to do with witchcraft again.

Ghyll had not seen how Demdyke had been flung into the fire and had not been there when she accused me. He told Nat she slipped, but he must have suspected something because I could see him looking anxiously at me as he said it. I kept quiet. I knew it was an evil thing and that evil would come of it.

The next morning, Demdyke came down from the hill to collect me.

'The girl is nothing of yours, wiseman,' she told Nat. She rolled up her sleeve and showed him the seared flesh of her arm. A great blister had sprung up along the whole of her forearm and onto her hand. 'There's no cures in her, this is harm she's done. She's one of us. I've come to take her.'

Nat looked at the wound. 'If it was harm it was not intended. There's no spite in our Issy.'

'She's one of us,' insisted Demdyke. 'You know nothing of her past. We will have her back.'

'What do you know of her past?' demanded Nat. I had told him what Demdyke had said about knowing my mother and grandmother. He also knew that she was a liar.

The old witch stood with one hand on Alizen's shoulder, her face lifted up to the sky. She always turned her face to the brightest part of the sky, to let a shadow of light into her dark world.

She shook her head at the sun. 'It's none of your business, wiseman,' she insisted. 'She dreams harm. She's one of us. We've been here longer than you, we will be here still when you and your church is forgotten and we will have what is ours. Give me the girl and we'll leave you alone.'

Nat shook his head. 'You'd make a slave of her. She's not mine to give or yours to take.'

Demdyke said, 'We're all slaves to our Master. But our Master will do as we ask him. Give me the girl or he will visit you.'

Nat shook his head. 'You can't harm me, witch. I don't believe in your charms.'

Demdyke waved her arm to the door where Ghyll and I were hiding. 'Ask your boy what I can do. Ask him what I have of his.' She nodded again to our hiding place. 'I'll come again. We will have her.'

She tapped her stick and Alizen turned to lead her away up the path back to Malkin Tower.

Ghyll turned to me as the witch disappeared up the hill. 'She means my mannikin. She has my soul. You have to go with her, Issy, or she'll kill me.'

*

'You have to choose between me and her, Father!' shouted Ghyll. His face had turned the colour of dead grass. 'She's not even our family, she's just an orphan. If she doesn't go, I'll die. Father, you have to listen to me!'

'She can't harm you,' Nat exclaimed for the tenth time. 'It's nonsense, she's trying to blackmail us. Do you expect me to give poor Issy to that monster because you're stupid enough to believe her?'

'But it's true,' groaned Ghyll. 'You can cure – she can make harm. Everyone knows it.'

'If she tries to make harm for you, I can cure you. What's the worry?'

'But she has my mannikin, she's trapped my soul, don't you understand?' Ghyll was weeping with fear. He really did believe his life was at stake.

'Mannikin!' scoffed Nat. 'Wax and a bit of hair. It's all hocus-pocus. All those spells and mannikins and charms and boiled-up messes – it's nonsense to frighten stupid children, like you!'

'But I felt the fire!' exclaimed Ghyll. 'She held my mannikin to the fire and I felt it.'

'You felt it because you believe it,' said Nat angrily. 'Some cunning man! You were born with gifts from God, but you've spent so long playing silly games, you've come to believe these tricks. Didn't I tell you to leave witchcraft alone? Now you want me to give away your sister to save you from your own stupidity.'

'But I do believe it, so it will happen. I can't help it,' wept Ghyll. 'And if it's just tricks, how did she know where I was hiding just now? Tell me that!'

'She knows because Alizen tells her. You saw how she stands with her hand on the Demdyke's shoulder. She taps in one place and it means over there . . . in another . . . over there. She gives the girl instructions before she sets out. It's an old trick.'

I sat by the corner near the fire and watched dumbly as Ghyll begged for my sacrifice. I felt worn out inside, but strangely removed from the scene, as if it were the fate of some other, strange girl that was being argued out.

'But how did she know where we were last night?' I asked. 'None of them could have known that.'

Nat had gone to fling more wood on the fire. He shrugged impatiently. 'Maybe she heard you, or even smelt you, like she made out,' he said. 'They say when you lose one sense the others make up for it. But I expect Jennet told her.'

I shook my head.

'I'm sorry, Issy. Maybe she's a darling like you say. You're a darling too, but you told Ghyll of her.'

I felt the truth of that. After all, I was no better than them.

'I will go with Demdyke if you want me to,' I said.

'She's one of them,' urged Ghyll. 'She burned

Demdyke.'

Nat was losing his temper. 'Your sister's no witch,' he shouted. 'It's tricks and lies. You know how these people work, what's wrong with you?'

'Her arm was burned, I saw it . . .'

'Tricks, just tricks,' insisted Nat. 'And if Issy does have gifts, what of it? So do I. Does that make me a witch – or you, for that matter?'

'But we cure. She brings harm,' begged Ghyll.

'Harm, is it?' he scoffed. 'Is it harm for her to save her brother from burning? I want to hear no more of it. Issy's staying.' He waved his hands in the air and went to get the big knife from its hook on the wall. He sat down and began to grind the blade with a piece of gritstone.

'I'll need your help today. We're going to butcher a pig this afternoon . . .'

'You see!' Ghyll jumped up crying. 'You see, she knew that too – she knows everything – what's the use, you won't listen . . . !' He burst into tears and ran out of the house crying. I could hear him wailing as he ran up the garden and away down the valley.

Nat sat down on a stool by the fire and rubbed his face wearily. 'So she knew I was going to kill a pig. So does half of Pendle,' he growled to himself.

'I won't let anything happen to Ghyll,' I said. 'He's your real son.'

He stroked my head. 'You're a daughter to me. I won't let you go.'

'But what happens if he falls ill? What happens

if he dies?'

'He won't fall ill,' Nat said. 'If he does, I'll cure him.'

'Demdyke has bewitched other people to death.'

'So they say,' growled Nat. He sighed and shook his head. 'He believes it, that's the trouble,' he muttered. 'And Old Demdyke knows it.'

That night, Jennet came to see me.

We had no windows, but she knew where I slept and I heard her scratching at the walls of timber and mud, calling my name. I ran to open the top of the door and she pulled herself up, leaning with her arms over it to peer in at me.

'I'm not allowed out,' I whispered to her. Nat had been called out to doctor Miller Bawdwin's family and he left strict instructions behind.

Jennet stared at me and smiled.

'It looks as though we're going to be sisters, now,' I said.

'Grandmother says you're a real witch to do what you did to her. She says none of the others could have done it, not even Mother.'

'I didn't mean to do anything – I don't know what I did. I was dreaming, I think,' I whispered back.

Jennet nodded. 'She says you wouldn't have got her if she'd known what a witch you really were,' she whispered. 'She says you belong at Malkin Tower with us. But I don't think so.'

'Don't you want me to come, Jennet?' I asked,

feeling a little put out. I had been thinking to myself that the only nice thing at Malkin Tower was that I would be with Jennet.

'You don't belong there.' She scowled. 'I used to think how you had such a pretty life with Nat and Ghyll but now you'll be up there with me and we'll both be miserable.'

'Could we run away?' I asked her. 'Demdyke won't hurt Ghyll if I'm not here.'

She shook her head. 'If you run away, she'll kill him.'

'But what about you? You can run away, even if I can't.'

'I can't,' she whispered. 'It's too late. They made me a witch. Demdyke says I mustn't make friends with Christians anymore. Tibb drank my blood and took away my soul. Look.'

She lifted her arm to show me the mark – a raw scab, surrounded by a small, blue bruise.

I thought of that creature feeding off her and shuddered. 'I'll have to do it, now,' I said.

Jennet didn't reply. We hugged one another. 'What are they doing to Ghyll?' I asked her after a while.

'Demdyke has a bowl of hot water and herbs, and she seethes him over it every morning to make him sick,' whispered Jennet. 'Is Ghyll here?' she added, peering past me into the darkness.

'No. Why?'

'I have to tell him,' replied Jennet simply, and added, 'You must tell him for me.'

I remembered that Nat said she might have given us away and I wondered if that was why she was really here tonight – to make sure Ghyll knew how he was being bewitched.

'Nat says it only works because he believes it,' I told her. 'Perhaps it's not a good idea to tell him.'

Jennet thought about this for a moment and then agreed.

I had an idea. 'Listen, Jennet – can you steal the mannikin for me? I'd do anything for you if you could . . .'

'Tibb drank my blood – I'm one of them,' she repeated. Then she kissed me. 'I have to go now.'

'Tell me one thing,' I pleaded. I felt awful for asking but I just had to know. 'Did you tell them we were coming that night?'

Jennet looked at me and said nothing. I babbled on, 'I wouldn't think any the worse of you, Jennet, because I told Ghyll, I gave you away first . . .'

Jennet's little white face looked over the stable door at me for a long moment but she said nothing. I couldn't tell if she was hurt or too guilty to admit it. Then she said again, 'I have to go now.'

She dropped down to the ground and I saw her running like a hare through the vegetable garden and away up the hill towards Pendle.

Nat returned from his work at the miller's looking grim. Bawdwin himself would never permit Nat to treat his family, but his wife believed that a cunning man was the only way to fight a witch's curse and she had asked him round while the miller was away on business. Bawdwin had turned Demdyke off his land a couple of days ago with a whip. Now, he had developed pains in his spine – what we called the Witch's Bolt. Nat could only treat him in person, but he was able to help his wife and daughter, who were suffering, too. The new baby was in the best of health. As Jennet had said, poor Alizen was not much of a witch.

The next day dawned mild under a dull grey sky. There was a warm little wind flicking in the thatch and Nat tried to rouse us to begin to prepare the land for the early seeds. We were taking out the tools when we heard voices outside. Demdyke had returned.

Alizen led her as usual. James was there, and Lizzie and a couple of other local witches. It was powerful harm that gathered so many together.

The witches sat themselves down on a ridge above our house, the wind stirring their rags. Nat took me by the hand and led me out to show we were not frightened, but Ghyll stayed and hid inside.

Demdyke took the little mannikin from her rags and held it up to be sure that we could see it. James had a little pot out and soon they had a small fire going, a flickering red flower in last year's old brown stalks. Water was added and some other things – a bundle of herbs and some other stuff I couldn't make out. Now, the fragrant smoke of the dry heather stems they used to make their fire was joined by a sickly reek, part sweet herbs and part some savoury smell like boiled meat, but not meat fit to eat. Over the simmering liquid in the pot they made a little nest of sticks, and on this laid the wax figure of Ghyll. Behind me, I heard the real Ghyll moan to himself.

'How's the boy this morning?' jeered Demdyke.

'As well as he is every morning.'

Demdyke stroked the little figure with her finger. 'He's getting hot,' she announced. 'Soon, he will begin to melt. When the wax is all in the pot, he will be dead. Give us the girl, wiseman.'

Nat did not reply but came back into the cottage. He sat down at his worktable and began to prepare some herbs for medicines.

Ghyll flung himself down on his bed in the corner. 'Why do they want her so much, Father?' he cried.

'I don't know, I don't know,' he snapped. And I saw him look at me in a way I'd not seen him look before – frightened and slightly distasteful, as if I were not quite human. For a second, I was a cuckoo in the nest, an overgrown monster, draining the life out of my adopted family. Then that fright in his eyes was gone and he was dear old Nat again.

For two hours that plume of sweet smoke and the stink of the witches' brew blew around our cottage. They sat on the ridge above us, muttering and mumbling their curses, occasionally shouting for Ghyll's benefit that the face was dissolving, or that poisonous matter was gathering in the eyes. At last they kicked out their fire and carried their things back up the hill, with a promise that they would be doing the same thing every day at that hour, back at Malkin Tower.

'In two weeks the boy will be dead,' announced Demdyke. She held up the little mannikin in the sunlight. Already the features were blurred.

The next morning, Ghyll had fever.

Chapter 7

A tiny, frozen bud was forming in my heart. The people I loved were being destroyed because of me but I felt nothing – no hope or fear for either myself or for Ghyll. I had lived for so long with the fear of myself and the threat of hell. It all seemed inevitable. Evil spread out of me in my breath. I had done everything the parson and Nat had told me to do – said my prayers, put the fire out of my mind, been a dutiful daughter. I loved my foster-father and brother and tried to look after them well. But none of it was any use. The blackness in my soul was seeping out, and nothing could stop it. I watched it with the same coolness as I might watch a pool of water oozing in a puddle across the floor.

I knew that in the end I would not let Ghyll die. If he did not get better, I would go to Malkin Tower.

Every morning when he knew that the witches were seething his mannikin over the fire, Ghyll grew a little worse. He refused even to try and fight the curse. He just lay there waiting, refusing to eat. He only spoke to beg that I go to them. He had made up his mind that he was bewitched, that he would be ill, and that the only cure was my sacrifice for him. Nat made medicines and did some of what he called hocus-pocus of his own. But the mannikin had taken a firm grip in Ghyll's imagination, and he couldn't shake its hold.

By the seventh day, Ghyll was very sick indeed. His temperature shot up, his breathing became bad, he ached all over and complained that his skin felt scalded. He could hardly bear to lie on his bed and kept moving this way and that, this way and that, trying to get comfortable.

He was almost triumphant about it. 'You see, you see,' he gasped. 'Nothing's working – Issy has to go to the witches, or I'll die. Two weeks she said . . .'

'You have to try,' pleaded Nat. 'You can't ask Issy to go there without even trying.'

But Ghyll was determined to be helpless. He grabbed my hand and put it on his hot head. 'You can feel it, I'm burning up,' he said eagerly. 'You have to go to them, Issy, you have to go.'

Nat said, 'No,' in a harsh voice. Ghyll lay back and turned his face to the wall. Nat went to sit in his corner by the fire and poked at it with a stick. I thought how small and old he seemed. None of his medicines or charms had even slowed down the course of the illness and he knew nothing more to help Ghyll. I went over to stand by him.

'He's a very sick boy, Issy,' he told me quietly . . .

I glanced over my shoulder. Ghyll had turned his head to watch us.

'If you tell me what to do, I'll do it,' I said at last.

Nat hesitated. 'If he dies,' he said, 'it will be hard for all of us. For you, too, Issy.'

'I know.'

All that week I had felt that hard column of ice growing inside me. I could not cry. I seemed to have no feelings, only that cold finger tight and hard in my chest. Sometimes it made it difficult even to speak and I found it impossible to meet the eyes of whoever was talking to me. Now Nat took my face gently in his hand and tilted it up to his. He peered seriously up at me, as if he wanted to see right into my heart. But I felt awkward and stiff, and tried to twist away.

'You seem so cold, now,' he scolded. 'As if you didn't care what happened to you anymore.' I shrugged. It was true.

Nat stared back into the fire. 'I don't know what to do,' he said. 'We can't let Ghyll die. But anything would be better than for you to spend your life with those creatures.'

He held his face in his hands and I could see the tears creeping through his fingers.

That afternoon the rain began. It poured down all afternoon and in the morning there was a constant heavy drizzle with no wind that seemed set to last all day. We had to postpone our work on the garden. We sat in the house with nothing to do, listening to Ghyll coughing and turning in his bed.

Shortly before midday a figure on horseback

appeared on the hillside above our house. He was dressed in waxed waterproofs and bent his head down over the horse to avoid the drips. It was Parson Holden. The parson liked his comfort, although he took his duties seriously, and I knew it could only be one thing to get him out on horseback from Colne in such wet weather.

He looked glumly at me while Nat hung his cape up to dry by the fire.

'How's the boy?' he asked.

'Bad, sir,' Nat said.

'I heard all about it.' He shook his head. 'There is a battle on for your soul, Isabel,' he told me. 'One small girl, but your soul is worth the same as any queen's. The Devil knows it and so does Demdyke. I've just come from her,' he said to Nat. 'You might be interested to know I offered her gold to give me the mannikin back, and she turned me down. She said Issy has powers even greater than her own.'

Nat turned his face away.

'I want a word with Issy.'

Nat nodded. 'I'll see to the horse, sir,' he said. He went outside to take the animal into our little barn and rub him down. Parson Holden took me by the hand and led me to sit by him at the table.

'Issy,' he said, 'is it true? Did you hex Demdyke?'

'I don't know,' I said with difficulty.

He leaned forward. 'Are you a witch, Issy?'

I said, 'No, sir,' but it was a lie. The truth was I didn't know.

'Have you been praying?' he asked.

'Every night.'

'Has God told you what to do?'

I shook my head.

'God has not helped you, then.' The parson frowned unhappily, but the fact that God had deserted me seemed to make up his mind. He took my hand. 'Issy,' he said, 'I do believe you are a witch.'

I stared down at the table. It never crossed my mind to doubt him. The parson was a man of God. If he said I was a witch, then I was. And yet I didn't hate God. I didn't love the Devil. It was like a terrible trick.

'Do I have to go to Malkin Tower?' I asked him shakily.

He shook his head grimly. 'You must come with me to see the magistrate and confess.'

I took my hand away. Was this his comfort? I didn't fear the law of God. Nat had brought me up to believe that I would be forgiven my sins if I repented. But I did fear the law of Man. I knew what they did to witches. Even a confessed witch had secrets in her heart that needed to be tormented out of her with fire and broken bones. In the end they were hanged. I didn't want to die. Above all I didn't want to die in the torture chamber under the magistrate's house in Colne.

Parson Holden was not a bad man. He had protected me over the years. I could see that he was frightened for me – and perhaps, of me.

I shook my head. 'Even you don't believe in me anymore . . .' I began tearfully, but he took my hand and shushed me.

'I believe you have a good heart,' he replied, 'but it means nothing. There are witches who work for the good, but still their souls are Satan's. The Devil prefers the bad but so long as he gets their souls in the end, why should he care? The Bible does not distinguish.' He quoted: ' "Thou shalt not suffer a witch to live." '

I had heard those words often enough from the pulpit of the church, or shouted at Demdyke in the streets. As he said them, he looked curiously at me.

'But, Parson, I never made a pact with the Devil,' I pleaded.

'We know nothing of your life before you came here,' he pointed out.

It was true, but even so – soul or no soul, witch or no witch, I would rather take my chances in Malkin Tower than end up in Lancaster Jail.

He knew what I was thinking. 'Are you frightened of dying, Issy?' he asked. 'God will help you to die if you confess. If you don't, there is hell in the hereafter.'

'Why should I fear hell?' I said bitterly. 'You know what they do to witches. There's always one last sin to drag out of them.'

He nodded. 'That's no small thing,' he said. 'But it may not come to that. What has happened to you isn't your fault – I'll testify to that. I know

Magistrate Nowell – he's an honest man. Issy, the witches in Pendle are finished. Bawdwin has gone over our heads to the Justice in Lancaster, and they've made him Witch-finder. He has permission to interrogate. You know what he is. No one is safe now. If you confess I can hope to save you. You've done no harm, you are ignorant of your circumstances – I'm sure you'll be let go. But if you wait for Bawdwin to take you – I know his sort. They like their work.'

'Sir . . . Do you really think you can save me?' I begged him.

He frowned. 'I can't promise. Bawdwin is determined. But, Issy, you know whatever they do to you, you cannot last long. Hell is forever. See . . .'

He took hold of the candle that was on the table between us and gave me a curious, sickly glance. Then he took my hand in his.

I guessed what was coming. I could see sweat on him. He didn't want to do it, but he had his duty to my soul, and to his.

'One small hand,' he said. 'In hell it will be your whole body. A few seconds. In hell, forever.' And he took my hand tightly in his two big ones and held my wrist over the candle flame.

I shrieked but he still held me tight. I began to howl and pull away, I clawed at his face but he was a strong man and he pulled me back into the flame.

'Confess,' he grated.

The door burst open. Nat dashed in, all the years shaken off him. He flung his hand across the priest's face, knocked him off his chair and onto the floor, and pulled me away. I backed into the wall and put my wound to my mouth.

Behind me the priest picked himself and wiped his mouth. There was blood in his beard. Nat took my hand and examined the burn.

'To do that to a child,' he cried. 'This is your God, is it?'

He could be thrown in jail and flogged for hitting Parson Holden, who looked stunned as he picked himself up. He was not used to this treatment. He looked at the blood on his hand. 'God will forgive you for striking a churchman,' he said thickly.

'But will he forgive you?' demanded Nat.

'It was my duty. My business is to take care of her soul, not her flesh.'

'Then leave her flesh alone!'

The priest frowned. 'This house is under a curse,' he said. 'I won't tell the magistrate that you struck me. I'll see you all in church on Sunday. I'll speak with Issy again then.' He took his cape and walked out into the rain.

Nat took my hand and examined the wound. There was a black ring with a red patch as big as my palm and the wound was already weeping.

'You must never fall into the hands of men like that,' said Nat bitterly.

Chapter 8

The next day was a Friday, the ninth of our bewitching. Ghyll had become delirious. I'd waited long enough.

I owned nothing but my bedding, my clothes, the doll Ghyll had made me and a pretty copper bracelet Nat gave me when I was ten. I left the bracelet behind because I knew it would be stolen at Malkin Tower. I left a set of clothes behind, too – smock, leggings and vest; I remembered what had happened to the vest I gave Jennet. All I had to do was wrap my doll in my leggings, my leggings in my smock and the whole lot in my blanket, and I had everything that was mine under my arm.

Outside blue sky was showing through the cloud. The breeze was blowing the smoke down through the smoke-hole, so that everything was cloudy and our sooty faces stung with the bitter blue smoke. Nat sat and stared at the fire as I packed my bundle. He said nothing.

I was quickly finished. I picked up the bundle and looked at him. I felt no pain or sorrow, just embarrassment. I waited awkwardly, not knowing how to say goodbye.

'Where are you going?' he said at last.

'Malkin Tower.'

He nodded. 'Better than to Lancaster Jail,' he

said. He stood up and tried to pull himself together. 'We'll tell Ghyll,' he said. 'Then we can have breakfast together – a good meal for you – you'll need it. I don't suppose there's much at Malkin Tower.'

Ghyll lay in a heap of blankets in the corner, behind a rug that Nat had hung from the wall to keep the smoke away. He stopped his muttering when Nat shook him awake and turned to look at us.

'I'm going today, Ghyll,' I said. 'Up to Demdyke. You'll be all right now.'

'You're really going?' he asked. I nodded. He grabbed my sleeve. 'Get the mannikin first,' he hissed. 'She'll cheat us. Get the mannikin first.'

Nat clapped his hands. 'That's right,' he exclaimed. 'It's a clear day today – they'll be out begging most likely. We'll go to Malkin Tower and bargain with them this evening. That means we've got hours yet – almost a whole day together, Issy.'

The thought that we had that time before us cheered us both up, as if my sentence to Malkin Tower was a lifetime away, rather than a few hours. Nat suddenly burst into life. He began to turn breakfast into a celebration.

There were some young pullets running around the yard, and he declared that we would have one for breakfast. He ran out into the yard to kill it and set me to plucking it while he built up the fire and baked some flat bread.

'Meat and bread and beer for breakfast, like two

fine gentlemen,' he cried. He drew a jug of ale – the good October beer, not the weak, small beer for everyday use, and we began tippling as we got ready. We both had empty stomachs, and I wasn't at all used to it – I was only allowed a small drop at festivals. Everything took on a carnival air – Nat singing his head off and pulling away at the bellows like a blacksmith, filling the whole cottage with gusts of thick blue smoke; me flinging handfuls of feathers around like confetti, and both of us dashing about for dripping pans, or the spit or just banging the pots together, a pair of delighted shadows in the thick smoke, coughing and wheezing and giggling as if we all had a birthday on the same day. Even Ghyll leaned up on one arm and grinned at the fun.

Nat cut the chicken up and spitted it and basted it in butter, and an hour after we'd been chasing it around the yard, we were dipping the hot bread into the dripping and smacking our lips. Ghyll couldn't stomach it and lay back in bed, muttering to himself again.

I stared at him, thin-lipped and pale, talking to no one, and I thought of Demdyke and the others waiting for me up on Pendle Hill. In that moment all the happiness ran right out of me, as if I were a pot with the bottom fallen out. I chewed at my meat and tried to look cheerful for Nat's sake. He winked at me over the top of his chicken leg. I thought I might never see that wink again and before I could stop myself, I began to cry.

Once the tears came I couldn't stop them. Our little show of happiness had melted that cold flower of ice in my heart and now I was myself again with nothing to hold me up and I just wept floods of tears, helpless to do anything to stop myself. Nat came round to comfort me.

'We were just showing off to ourselves, weren't we?' he murmured. He held me while I cried myself out. 'We have to be practical about it,' he said at last. 'We'll look about and see what we can find for you to take along . . . Maybe some presents for them . . . they might treat you better if they think you'll bring them things. I've some old clothes you can take. But first, let's eat our chicken. You'll need something in your stomach today, even if you don't feel like it.'

We did our best with that bird, but neither of us had much of an appetite. Afterwards, Nat got up and began ransacking the house in an effort to find things for me to take.

There was precious little at this time of year. He found some cheese and the end of last year's bacon, some vegetables stored from last autumn and a few handfuls of dried peas. I didn't want him to give away what he really needed. Things would be more useful to me in the house where it would not be stolen and I could at least run down and take some. When we'd finished we sat inside with Ghyll. We had hours to go before the witches came back from their begging. Nat tried to take my mind off it, but it was no use. Ghyll muttering away in his corner reminded me of Demdyke, the burn on my arm reminded me of the hell-fire the parson had promised me. Nat suggested we do some work preparing herbs for medicines to take our minds off it.

We worked steadily away, sorting out seeds and leaves, grinding, mixing and cutting until lunch time. I was actually beginning to long for the evening so that the ordeal of waiting would be over and I could begin my new life. Nothing could make the time pass quickly. We sat together at the little table, stirred at our messes of gruel with our spoons, staring down and not looking at each other.

I was fighting back my tears and Nat had pushed away his plate and was fingering a lump of bread when someone pushed the door open abruptly and walked in.

She was a tall, plump woman, dressed in a long waxed cape and with proper leather boots on her feet. She was covered in mud from head to toe. She'd obviously come a long way on foot.

'Issy is in trouble,' she said. It was not a question, but a statement. She peered down through the smoke at our faces. 'What a miserable-looking pair!' she exclaimed. She opened her mouth wide in delight, and let out a long gurgling laugh that made us both smile at her despite everything. She kicked off her boots and came in with no invitation to join us on the bench, pulling off her leather gloves.

She offered me her hand, still concealed by a thin woollen under-glove. 'Iohan a-Style,' she said. She held her hand out to Nat and giggled at his expression, which had changed from one of total misery to one of total surprise. 'That bundle of rags has come a long way since I gave her to you in Colne market street, wiseman.' She grinned at me and nodded towards Nat. 'I made a good choice, didn't I, Issy?'

She sat down, gurgled her curious, bubbling laugh again and said, 'Now, tell me all about it. What's wrong with the boy?'

Iohan a-Style had no grand manners, but you couldn't help but be impressed by her. She listened to our story with a practical air, as if she were a carpenter being given instructions for a table or a chair. But there was an intensity about her and you felt that all her body and soul was occupied in sitting there and listening.

'We must get the mannikin back, then,' she said when he had finished.

'They won't part with it, not for gold,' said Nat.

Iohan twisted her bag off her back and patted it. 'There are things witches love more than gold. And things they fear, if I have to use them.' I looked curiously at the bag, but she caught my eye and shook her head. 'But first, I have to ask another favour, wiseman. I've come a long way on oat cakes and water.' She turned her head and smiled fondly at the chicken on the table.

As she ate I watched her. She smiled and winked. How had she known I was in trouble? What was I to her that she had travelled so far on foot in stinking weather to rescue me? I remembered that Demdyke had called me – 'Isabel a-Style'.

This woman shared my name.

That evening, Iohan set off on foot up to Malkin Tower to bargain with the witches for Ghyll's life and my soul. She flung her bag over her shoulder and patted it with a smile. I wondered again what she had in there and she seemed to know what I was thinking, because she winked at me and said, 'Two pounds of Cod's-wallop and a powdered toad.'

I laughed at that, but Nat didn't look at all happy.

'It takes a witch to deal with a witch,' he muttered as we watched her trudge up the muddy path to Pendle Hill. He looked sideways at me. 'God will forgive us for accepting her help today.'

She was only gone a few hours. She walked right into the house again without knocking, put down her bag by the door, reached into her cape and brought out the mannikin.

Ghyll's hair was twisted about it but it had melted away until all that was left was the vague outline, as much like a candle as a human figure.

'The most expensive candle I ever bought,' remarked Iohan. But she didn't tell us what she'd paid. 'It doesn't look much like him, does it?' she added, and she grinned. 'I think a bit of cheating wouldn't go amiss.'

She went over to the fire to warm the mannikin up, and then set to work on it. She pinched and pulled and a few seconds later held it out again. She had remodelled Ghyll's face.

'Hocus-pocus,' she gurgled happily.

Ghyll was very sick, and Nat was half convinced it was already too late. Iohan had no such doubts. She put the mannikin into his hands and watched while he examined it carefully. At last he nodded, sighed, cradled it to his breast and closed his eyes to go to sleep.

Iohan got down on her knees by his side and felt his head, then his pulse. 'We'll have another look at him in an hour or so and see if he needs any help,' she said. 'And now . . . I've been travelling for two days and I've not had a wink. Where can I sleep?'

Nat showed her his bed. She fell straight into it, pulled the blankets over her and in another second began snoring loudly. Nat and I looked at one another in amazement.

'Well,' he said. 'That's that . . . I suppose!'

Chapter 9

Iohan took over our house entirely. As soon as she woke up she sent a lad from down the road to the baker to order a cake, got Nat to kill another chicken, which he certainly could not afford, and declared grandly that today was a feast day. She'd brought nuts and sweets and candied fruits with her and we picked at them while everything was got ready.

Nat was grateful for what she had done, of course, but I could see he wasn't happy about his guest. She refused to tell us how she had won the mannikin back – 'There are some things it's better not to know,' she said – and he suspected her of knowing more than a little witchcraft herself. When she offered to doctor Ghyll Nat refused and tended him with his own herbal remedies. Iohan just shrugged. But she suggested that I help him in the curing.

Nat looked at her. 'I have no such gifts . . .' I began to explain. But Iohan shook her head.

'You have more than you know,' she told me. And I saw Nat look at me again with that suspicious glance. He treated Ghyll while the chicken was roasting, and Iohan took me outside and insisted that I show her the wound on my arm where the parson had burned me. I had lost an area of skin as big as my palm, and Iohan scowled angrily as she examined it.

'He preaches love with this hate in his heart,' she growled.

'It was for my own good – the parson is a good man,' I insisted. 'He wanted me to confess but I wasn't brave enough.'

'Good, you call him?' snorted Iohan. 'Then God protect this land until it learns what goodness is.' She put her hand over the wound. I remember thinking it was odd that that didn't hurt it. She smiled and said, 'It'll be better soon – but you'd better keep the bandage on a while in case Nat sees.'

She went inside to turn the chicken. I didn't know what she was talking about; the wound was still there. Only that night when I went to bed did I realise that I hadn't noticed my hurt arm for hours, and when I took the bandage off it had healed right over in those few hours. I did as she asked, though, and kept the bandage on.

The chicken was soon ready, and the day after Iohan had walked down from the hill with Ghyll's mannikin in her cloak, we were all sitting around the table to eat chicken and cake with cream. The meal began awkwardly. Nat was growing more and more suspicious of his guest, but Iohan was so full of fun that Nat just couldn't help himself and we spent the meal roaring with laughter. Ghyll perked up, too, and although he was still weak he got up to sit at the table and eat some broth and a little bread. Iohan did a wonderfully funny impersonation of Demdyke boiling up the mannikin, and she had him in such fits of laughter with it, you'd never believe that the old witch had very nearly frightened him to death.

After dinner Iohan announced she had some presents. Once again she turned to her bag.

'Something to help the cunning man in his trade,' she said. Nat looked alarmed and I could see he thought she was going to bring out some piece of witchery. She made that long, gurgling laugh of hers and told him not to worry, she'd left all the oddities up at Malkin Tower.

She'd brought a pestle and mortar for Nat, a good clay one.

Nat thanked her and stroked the smooth clay bowl with his finger. 'It's much better than my old one,' he admitted.

'Not much payment for looking after Issy for ten years,' commented Iohan.

For Ghyll she had a little knife with a sickle-shaped blade and a horn handle. 'For cutting herbs,' she said. 'There's also this.' She handed him a little polished red stone on a silver chain. 'This is a charm against witchcraft,' she told him. 'Demdyke knows you're frightened of her and she'll try again. This will help. You nearly lost your life and cost your sister her soul,' she added severely. 'Keep to the herbs in future.'

'I promise,' muttered Ghyll.

'Now for Issy,' said Iohan. She took out of her bag a cape, just like hers, waxed and long and with ties right down the front, and a pair of real leather boots, iron shod to grip the ground.

'We have a long journey before us,' said Iohan. 'I want Issy to come with me.'

I jumped up – frightened or excited, I don't know which.

'Where? When?' I wanted to know. But Nat waved his hand for me to sit down.

'But she wants me . . .' I began. Nat gave me a sideways glance that shut me up.

'This is her home, now,' he said. 'I can't afford to let her go.'

'You have Ghyll,' said Iohan. 'I daresay your daughter Kate will help out.'

Iohan seemed to know everything without being told. Nat scowled.

'You gave her into my care,' he pointed out. 'She's not yours to take back.'

Iohan nodded agreement. 'But there are things she needs to learn.' She looked across the table to me. 'What do you remember about your life before you came here, Issy? she asked.

Then I told her about my dream. I could see Nat frowning at me. It was an unspoken rule that these things should never be mentioned, but there was something about Iohan that brought all my secrets tumbling out of me.

'I know where that dream comes from and I can help you to understand it, when the time is right,' said Iohan. 'I promise you that neither of us has anything to do with hell or the Devil or harm of any kind.' She looked seriously into my face. 'When I knew you, you had gifts, God-given gifts of healing and seeing. I can help you get them back. Such gifts will grow, whether you want them or not. You must be careful they grow properly. You have a bad name here for no fault of your own. Even to be a wiseman is dangerous these days. Demdyke is interested in you, so is the parson. They are dangerous people, and there are others worse. It would be better to come now, for a while anyway, until this business is forgotten. Remember,' she smiled, 'you can leave me whenever you like. Nothing's forever. With your father's permission of course.'

Nat gave me another hot little glance. I knew that he loved me, but he was thinking that I was dangerous to him, his family and myself, and he was no longer able to protect me.

'It's up to our Issy,' he growled.

I knew then that he had let me go.

Chapter 10

I was to have a new life after all. Nat didn't trust Iohan but I thought she was wonderful. She'd saved me and Ghyll, she'd cured my burn – and she was so brimming over with life and fun. I told myself not to be so pleased about it – that Nat knew best, that I was leaving my family behind, that I was going off with a stranger who knew the ways of witches. But it made no difference. Iohan had melted me. I just wanted to smile every time she came into the room. I'd fallen in love with her.

She was in a great hurry to get away and we left first thing the next morning. Ghyll was asleep, still very weak from his illness, but Nat got up and cut bread for us. 'I'll send word to you if I can,' he said. 'Come back to us, won't you, Issy?' I nodded and felt like crying. He wanted to change the dressing on my arm, but Iohan said she'd done it earlier. Nat gave me a funny look, but he didn't press. Then he kissed me goodbye and we set off across the wooden bridge over the stream behind the house, past the little coppice that shielded us from the wind and provided our firewood, and up over the hills towards Hebden Bridge. The ground was still very wet underfoot, but a brisk wind was beginning to dry the wet leaves and the grass.

We had been out of the house for no more than a couple of minutes when the first strange thing happened. We were walking out from the coppice into the fields when a tiny black figure ran helter-skelter out of the bushes and stopped in the road, shrieking angrily at Iohan in no language I'd ever heard. He was no more than a few centimetres high and I was so shocked that I screamed in alarm.

'Get away with you,' said Iohan quietly. And suddenly it was nothing more or less than a blackbird, which had jumped out of the bushes to scold us. Now it flew off into a tree and I could hear it calling in alarm. Iohan turned to smile at me, and then carried on up the hill. I just stood there, my heart beating away from the shock. I heard feet and Nat ran up behind me.

'What is it?'

'. . . I thought I saw something . . .'

Poor dear Nat was ready to fight a dragon for me at that second and I brimmed over with love for him. We stood looking at each other for a moment and I was ready to run back into his arms. But then I heard Iohan call, already well on her way up the hill and I turned without thinking and ran after her. When I looked back a dozen steps further on, he was already gone.

The way was slippery with mud from all the rain and we worked our way slowly up towards the top without a word. I was sleepy when we set out but now my mind was racing. Surely the blackbird was just my mind playing tricks? But I wasn't sure. Iohan had plenty of mysteries about her and I began to realise I had a thousand questions to ask.

When we got near the top of the hill and the ground levelled out, I ran to catch up with her to ask her about something that had been on my mind ever since she first walked through the door.

'Iohan . . . Iohan . . .' She stopped and let me draw level. 'How did you know I was in trouble?' I begged.

She leaned confidentially over to me. 'My imp told me,' she whispered. I must have looked terrified, because her eyebrows shot up with delight and she roared with laughter.

'Cod's-wallop!' she shouted, and roared with laughter again, just at the sound of that word. She lifted her hands to her face and shouted, 'Cod's-wallop!' again and again, up to the sky, and across the dales over to Pendle Hill, lying like a great animal on the horizon behind us. 'Cod's-wallop! Cod's-wallop!' she yelled, laughing and gurgling like a drain, until I began to laugh too, and I shouted it after her – 'Cod's-wallop! Cod's-wallop!' over and over until we were both sick of laughing.

When at last we stopped she rubbed her sides and complained that she hurt with laughing. She said, 'We mustn't do that too often, or we'll have no strength for the walk.' Then she added, 'Sometimes I just know things about people, especially people I care for.' She raised her eyebrows at me and stuck her stick in the ground, and we carried on toiling slowly up the wet hill.

Our walk began under a bright sky and a cool wind, perfect weather for walking. But the ground underfoot was sodden and we were often struggling in the mud. We might have had a lift with a wagon but the roads below were just rivers of mud at this time of year and Iohan preferred to stick to the footpaths. When we passed above a big road we could see the wagons up to their axles in mud, the horses and mules slipping and slithering and sitting down, their legs and flanks covered in it as if they had swum in it. The paths across the hills and dales were too narrow and high for the wagons to pass, but even these were often calf-deep in wet, sticky mud. Most people had to walk if they wanted to get anywhere and by the spring after a wet winter the paths were little more than bogs. My boots were soon great balls of mud. Some of the ways were used by pack horses, carrying goods to and fro across the dales. The powerful, steady Galloway horses used for this work carried everything on their backs across the moors – coal, stone, iron, fleeces. But their commonest load was lime from the quarries at Clitheroe, and we were so used to seeing the white, lime-dusted rows of horses snaking their way along the valley sides that they were known locally as Lime Gals. They made the ways impassable, and we footwalkers set up a separate path for ourselves to one side of the main passage.

*

Although I saw nothing strange after that first vision in the coppice, Iohan very often made odd remarks to the things of the countryside around her.

'It's all very well for you,' she said at one point, as we crossed a boggy patch of land on a high flat hill. I looked up to see who she was talking to, but there was nothing there but a bright green patch of moss to one side of the path. 'I prefer it a bit drier, myself,' she added, nodding in a friendly manner at the moss before she carried on. I thought it was just her sense of humour, except she wasn't laughing.

Another time as we began to climb up to the moors after Marsden village she began a conversation with a clump of heather.

'That's bad luck,' she remarked suddenly.

'What is?' I asked.

She pointed to the heather. 'It's the white flowered type,' she said, adding to the heather, 'You'll just have to live with it.'

I looked doubtfully at the plant, which didn't look any different from any other heather to me. It wasn't in flower. I asked her how she knew it was a white one.

'It told me,' said Iohan, smiling. I thought she might start shouting Cod's-wallop again, but she didn't add anything and began to walk off.

'But I thought white heather was supposed to be lucky,' I panted, struggling to keep up with her.

'Not for the heather it isn't,' pointed out Iohan. She smiled and chuckled. 'Right next to the footpath, too. It's always getting picked. The poor thing hasn't set seed in four years.'

These events made me even more curious. Iohan kept up a good pace and I didn't have much breath for questions. When I did ask she always managed to put me off, saying there was plenty of time for that later on, or just by walking faster.

I had to put up with that, but she couldn't stop me thinking. Shortly after lunch I remembered something that stopped me dead in my tracks. Iohan was walking rapidly along a stony little path by a brook and didn't seem to notice how struck I was.

'Iohan!' I shouted.

She took no notice at all and began to disappear round a corner. I yelled, 'Iohan!' again and ran after her, really angry with her for ignoring me.

She turned and waited for me.

'Are you . . .' I drew up with her but I felt foolish suddenly.

'Well?'

'Are you my mother?'

'Your mother?' Her eyebrows shot up. 'Why should you think that?'

I had remembered what Old Demdyke had said that time by the fire – that my name was a-Style. 'And your name is a-Style, too, isn't it? I said.

'Old Demdyke knows a little of something and a lot of nothing. She knows of me and she knows my name, and she wanted to impress you. Your name isn't a-Style, nothing like it. As for me, I'm Widow a-Style. My husband Tom a-Style died five years ago.'

She smiled sadly, and then turned round to continue walking. I paused for a moment, before realising that she had still told me nothing of what I really wanted to know – myself.

'Then what have you got to do with me?' I demanded.

Iohan shrugged and carried on walking.

'Iohan!' I was infuriated. 'Iohan! I want to know – where did I come from? I don't know anything about myself. What happened to my mother? Who am I?' I wailed, in tears of frustration.

She turned to face me. 'You know,' she said.

'But I don't know, I don't know anything.' I stamped my foot I was so cross and splattered both of us with muddy water.

Iohan ignored the mud and stared intently at me. 'You know,' she insisted. 'You told me yourself.'

'When? How? I don't understand – I don't remember anything.'

'I won't tell you anything – nothing at all,' she promised. 'But I will help you remember.'

What with the mud, and slipping in it and falling in it and toiling through it, we made slow progress. We didn't get much beyond Marsden that first day, and we slept in a small barn above the village. We awoke at first light when the yeoman came round on his morning chores. Iohan yawned, crawled out from under her heap of straw and went to peer outside. I heard her cursing. The breeze was gone and a silent drizzle like a wet mist fell out of the motionless air.

We helped the yeoman with his chores, sweeping the yard and feeding the chickens and the pigs, although he wouldn't let us milk the ewes or collect the eggs, in case we stole them, I suppose. But he gave us some milk to drink, still warm from the ewes, and Iohan bought two small flat cheeses from him before we carried on our way. Already the rain was heavier and a wind began to blow from the north-west.

I was feeling sulky and cross with Iohan. She had spoiled my hopes that I would find out about myself. I was certain I knew nothing, despite what she said and I thought she was playing some kind of silly game. As the day went on the wind blew harder, the rain got heavier and colder and the paths became more slippery and deeper in mud. I was unused to this kind of effort. The sheer hard work of moving forward, and the cold and the rain finding its way through my clothes pushed all my questions to the back of my mind. We stopped and had lunch sheltering in a shepherd's hut, and then set off across the high moorland. Up here, the wind began to rush past us in great, cold gusts. We were walking directly into it and I was soon exhausted.

We were coming up over a rise when we were caught in a cloudburst. The rain fell in bucketfuls and the wind whipped it up in all directions. In a few seconds we were both drenched right through. My new cape did nothing to stop it; my boots were sodden inside and out and I felt utterly miserable, wet through, cold, hungry, tired and useless for anything.

Iohan reached the bottom of a slope and turned to watch me moil through the mud towards her. As I drew up with her I slipped and fell on my backside in the middle of a puddle. Iohan's eyebrows went up in delight. 'What a mess,' she gurgled. I must have looked truly ridiculous, because she began to laugh, gurgling and snorting and bending over, laughing all the more as I just sat there up to my middle in water. I tried to stand but fell back and finally I began to cry. Iohan stopped laughing and came over to help me up.

'Come on,' she encouraged me. 'It's too far in one go for a wee slip like yourself. I'll tell you what . . . since you're to be my own girl henceforth, we'll celebrate by spending a night in an inn.' She pointed over the rise. 'There's one I passed a couple of miles up the dale . . . that'll do us. There's a girl, you can make a couple of miles I expect, if there's a fire and a hot supper at the end of it.'

I tried again to stand up in my puddle, but I was still crying and two miles might have been the moon as far I was concerned. Iohan hauled me out, set me on the road and then marched off into the rain, making encouraging noises. But she'd taken no more than a couple of steps when she too suddenly skidded, her legs shot up in the air, her skirts flying round her head, and she fell with a great splash in the middle of a deep puddle. She sat there with her legs stretched out and the water flowing past her, gurgling happily to herself, and she looked so ridiculous I had to laugh too.

'That's just what you did yourself,' she chortled. I forgot all about my tears and went to help her up, but she grabbed my hand and pulled me in again, and we both giggled and flapped about in the water like a pair of overdressed frogs. Those last two miles to the inn went quickly after that. Only later did I realise that she'd fallen in on purpose just to cheer me up.

By the time we got to the Pack Horse Inn we were a pair of great bundles of filthy sodden rags, and the innkeeper looked very doubtfully at us when Iohan announced that she wanted a room for the night. Even when she jangled her purse at him, he still didn't like the idea. But when she said, 'Mistress a-Style of Hebden Bridge. It would be better to let me in,' he opened the door quickly enough. It was clear from his look that he didn't like it one little bit.

The inn was busy with shepherds driving their flocks to market and yeoman farmers or their men taking fleeces to be sold. Iohan managed to get us a little room to share with a couple of other women. She ordered a great tub of scalding hot water in which we bathed one after the other, while our spare clothes, which were as wet as we were, dried in front of the fire. They were still damp when we put them on, but we were at least warm as every room in the inn had a great wood fire blazing away.

Then we went down for a hot meal of stewed mutton. I ate meat rarely and I was ravenously hungry. We both ate two helpings with fat slices of coarse barley bread and sweet butter.

After the meal, Iohan dragged me across into a crowd of herders who had taken over the fireplace. She pushed her way towards the fire – 'On account of the girl, who needs a spot of warmth.' The herders grumbled about being ousted like that, but they were a good-natured bunch, and Iohan was so cheery that they soon forgot about it and began talking sheep again.

The herders not only talked sheep, they smelt of them too. As they crowded close to the flames they steamed and stank until my eyes began to water. Iohan told them it was enough to drive a witch off, and they laughed. She declared the air was so wet with the steam that we'd be drier out of it, and so we pushed our way out of the crowd again and headed off into a smaller back room that was nearly empty. We got ourselves the fireside settle. Iohan ordered mulled small ale and we warmed our toes in the cinders and drank our beer.

Now that I was warm and fed, my curiosity came flooding back. Apart from the infuriating remark that I already knew who I was, I had learned nothing in two days of being with Iohan – except that my name was not a-Style, which was hardly great progress. I glanced across at her. Since she had said that she would tell me nothing, I decided not to ask her about myself or about her. Instead, I asked her how she had got the mannikin off Demdyke.

Iohan sighed. 'It's always questions with you. Why don't you just drink your beer and shut your face for a bit, hey?' She took a long swig of her ale and tucked her mug to keep warm by the fireside.

'I might as well, you never give me any answers,' I complained.

'I'm not very full of answers, it's true,' she admitted. She took up her mug again, holding it under her chin in her gloved hands. I realised I had never seen her without those thin woollen gloves. I suppose she must have taken them off for the bath, but somehow I had not seen her hands.

'The mannikin,' she murmured thoughtfully. She began to drink again, but something seemed to be amusing her, and she began to splutter in her beer.

'The mannikin,' she giggled, wiping her mouth. 'Well, I don't like questions and answers, but I do like a story so I'll tell you. I paid Demdyke one farthing for it and she was as happy as a sparrow.'

'But Parson Holden offered her gold . . .' I began.

'I found the old place – Malkin Tower, isn't it? – and the old girl was sitting outside sucking a bone. I told her I was a witch, like herself, and that I'd come that way to help my aunt, who lived in Marsden. She wanted to know who this aunt was, so I gave her some nonsense about an old widow who lived on her own – you get half a dozen in every village. Of course, her sort have to pretend they know everything and sure enough she said she knew who I meant. Then I gave her a tale about the yeoman wanting this aunt of mine off his land and me needing some wax to model him with, to give the man a scare so he'd lay off her. Demdyke was willing enough to sell to me – although she drove a hard bargain, given that she thought I was one of her own. I thanked her very nicely, went halfway back and made that little model I gave to poor Ghyll.'

'You mean it wasn't the real mannikin?' I began to panic. 'But what about Ghyll . . .?'

Iohan growled, 'One old hag tricked him into being ill; another old hag tricked him out of it. That's all there is to it.'

'But she'll come again and show him the real mannikin.'

Iohan shrugged. 'That's his lookout. I told him she'd still try her tricks on him. He won't know what to believe. That'll be enough to stop her in her tracks.'

'But . . . then why did you re-model the face when you got back to us? – Ghyll didn't know about that at all.'

'I wanted Nat to believe it was the real one – and you, too, for that matter. Old Demdyke had the whole lot of you charmed up to the eyeballs – a bigger houseful of babies I've never come across,' complained Iohan breezily. 'Besides, what do you think Nat'll do when Demdyke comes round waving her mannikin about the place and Ghyll starts having doubts? He'll tell him how I redid the face while he was asleep, of course, and that'll make it seem all the truer, won't it?'

Iohan always seemed to have an answer for everything, but sometimes I could swear she was making it up on the spot. But the fact was, mannikin or not, Ghyll had been better when we left the house.

'The joke is,' beamed Iohan, 'that I bought the wax to do it off Demdyke herself. She'll be furious when she finds out – furious!' She gurgled with laughter and stretched her bare toes into the ashes. 'I'm a clever old girl, you have to give me that,' she boasted.

'But then – are you . . .'

'Am I what?'

'Are you – are you a witch?'

'A witch? Like Old Demdyke? Wax figures and smelly brews and baby's fat and all that? Cod's-wallop!' she said again, and smiled.

I began to speak but . . . 'That's enough!' She flapped her hands at me. 'I told you, I don't like questions and answers – I don't agree with them, for a start. I'm not going to answer anymore. But what I will do – if you can guess the answer before you know what the question is, I'll let you know if you got it right.' She took a long pull from her mug and her bright eyes twinkled at me over the rim, daring me to ask what on earth that was supposed to mean.

Chapter 11

Iohan decided I wasn't strong enough to carry on on foot, so she paid a man for the hire of a pony and I came to her house in fine style – my first time ever on horseback.

Iohan had a large cottage in over an acre of land, spotted around with little sheds and outhouses. Unlike Nat, she owned the land, and as well as keeping pigs, chickens, ducks and geese, she even grazed a cow on her neighbour's field. The cottage was a stone building – another sign that she was well off. The stone was undressed and held together by thick, coarsely-smeared mortar, but the walls were thick, solid and dry. She even had a little chimney poking out of the roof, and so the inside wasn't filled with smoke all the time as ours was.

Iohan's house had three rooms – one for her, one for the animals and another packed from floor to eaves with bales of cloth. There were various lean-tos added on, and many of these as well as the little outhouses were filled with cloth as well. It seemed that Tom a-Style had been a cloth merchant, and Iohan kept the business up. She did all the buying and selling and there was a man, Tolly, who ran the place while she was away and helped her while she was at home. There was a boy, Mark, to run errands. She also paid a girl to look after the garden and the animals and do the housework. Iohan didn't have to lift a finger if she didn't want to. I could never make up my mind whether she was lazy or busy, because she would spend some days in bed till lunch time, and others up at dawn working until dusk.

She made it clear right from the start that she expected me to work for my keep. Her girl, Joan, was not at all friendly and I found out why a couple of mornings later when Iohan woke me at four to milk the cow and sheep. I asked where Joan was.

'We don't need her so long as you're here,' Iohan replied.

I felt sorry for Joan, although I learned later that Iohan had good reason for getting rid of her.

Taking over Joan's job made life at Iohan's not much different from life at home. Sometimes, when business was brisk, I helped with the cloth, but most of my work was done in the garden.

Iohan's garden was like a green cloak laid on the side of the valley where she lived. You could see it from miles off, standing out against the dull winter grass of the pastures. I noticed it when we came down off the tops on our arrival, but when I actually got down to working on it I realised how far ahead it was. In our little garden back in Pendle we were just watching the first seeds come through and protecting delicate things from frost. Here I found myself planting out stout little seedlings, picking leafy vegetables and watching the first beans come into flower. The garden was in a sheltered spot and it got the sun from dawn to dusk, but even these advantages couldn't explain how she could grow things like peaches and melons, which I had only ever heard of before and were normally grown under glass in the big houses of the rich.

Things in the garden grew faster than I would have thought possible, and she could have lived off that one acre, had she wanted to. But her main business was the cloth. She provided yarn to over a hundred weavers, bought the finished cloth from them and transported it on horseback every week to the Saturday market at Halifax. Every day, weavers were coming and going with pieces of coarse woollen fabric balanced on their heads and shoulders to sell. Iohan would get Mark to pour out some beer and sat in the garden with them to haggle over the price. I heard complaints that she was stingy with her money. It seemed that Iohan was the only cloth merchant for miles and if she struck a hard bargain the weavers had no choice but to take it. On the other hand, everyone agreed she was generous with loans or even gifts of money if they fell sick. She was generous enough to me. Shortly after we arrived she gave me a couple of silver coins and said they were mine. I had never seen so much money all together. I wrapped it up in a scrap of cloth and hid it in my bundle. I planned to give it to Nat when I went back home.

Iohan had other interests as well as cloth. She was certainly a wise-woman – she admitted that openly. People often came to see her for cures for their families and animals. She had a little hut in the garden where she took people to treat them. Once she asked me to come and help her.

'You have the gift, too,' she said. But I shook my head. That was one gift I didn't want. It seemed safer that way.

There were other mysteries about her that were not so easily explained. The one that troubled me most was the fact that she disappeared every Thursday night, from late evening until dawn the next day, and she spent all of Friday morning in bed. I discovered that Tolly disappeared too. I knew that Thursday was the witches' day – the day they held their Sabbat in honour of the Devil. But of course I did not believe such a thing of Iohan and I tried to convince myself that she had a lover or some other secret not so dark.

Iohan still refused to answer any of my questions. She insisted that I knew the answers myself and that if she told me I would never learn how to find things out for myself.

'Not a single question will I answer,' she told me. 'But I will show you how to look, when the time is right.'

That meant nothing to me and I was beginning to start wondering if there were things she didn't want me to know when she gave me my first lesson.

*

We had spent the morning pulling down an old chicken shed that had not been used for some years. We heaped this up in the middle of the garden with some other rubbish and started a fire. The wood was damp, but even so Iohan quickly got up a good blaze. She stood watching the flames leap in the air, but I as always felt uncomfortable near fire. I felt the scars on my face beginning to itch and I turned away.

Iohan took my hand. 'Wait with me,' she said.

I pulled back.

'You can go when you like. But there's something for you here.'

I let her lead me back to the fire. The flames jumped and fluttered.

'Fire holds a secret for you,' said Iohan. 'This is where you have to learn about yourself . . . this is where the answers to your questions lie . . . in the heart of the fire. Can you be brave?'

I said, 'I don't know.' I didn't feel brave.

'I promise it won't hurt. But you will be frightened. I want to teach you how to look into the fire. Will you try?'

Against my will I nodded.

She squeezed my hand. 'Stay very still, very still,' she whispered. 'I want you to look into the fire, right into the heart of the fire. It's all right, I'll hold you if you feel faint. Think of nothing and let your mind go quiet, as if you were going to sleep . . .'

The flames pounding and beating in the air, the warmth on my face, her voice, whispering, whispering inside me . . . I grew still and calm as if I were watching all this from a great distance. Gradually garden, Iohan, even the fire, disappeared altogether and I was in a warm, snug, dark place, safely tucked out of all harm's way. Only the beating of the flames in the air remained, regularly pulsing, throbbing, shaking the air . . . then I became aware of a murmuring all around me and someone shouting my name . . .

That warm bubble ruptured. Someone grabbed hold of me and I was tossed to and fro in the air. Then a ferocious blast of heat, a terrible searing blow of pain on my face and hands . . . and there was the fire before me, a huge roaring fire that lunged up to the sky. Someone held me in a solid grip before it. I tried to move my head, but could not. I tried to wriggle and to scream but every time I took a breath a blast of hot air burned my throat. I was suffocating, I was burning alive . . .

From far away there was a voice, a whisper speaking to me, telling me something. Desperately, I turned to it. It was Iohan. As I recognised her I realised that this was only a dream, that it could not harm me; but that did not make the pain or the terror any the less at that moment. She was telling me to be still, to stay dreaming, to remember the fire-dream right through to its end. I tried to listen through the choking and the burning . . .

'Open your eyes, Issy . . . see into the fire . . . look . . . what do you see in the fire . . .?'

'I can't!' I moaned. But I couldn't help myself. My eyes opened against my will; there was the face and I screamed and screamed and screamed and . . .

Everything vanished suddenly. I was back in the garden, staggering away from the fire. I turned from the blaze and fell gasping to the ground.

Immediately she was there with me, holding me in her arms. 'There's a girl, Issy, well done, well done. You're with me now, it's all right now,' she said, cradling me in her arms.

'I dreamt,' I panted.

She shook her head. 'Not a dream. A memory.'

I touched the scars on my face. 'I had an accident . . .'

She shook her head again. 'Not just an accident.'

'But I was only two years old. No one can remember that far back.'

'You can – you just showed it. Did you look, Issy? Did you see into the fire?'

'A face . . .'

'What face?'

I pushed her away and tried to stand up. I shook my head to shake that memory away. 'I can't remember – I always forget the face . . .'

'You have to remember the face, Issy, you have to remember what happened to you that day. It's the only way for you to know.' She used the words 'to know' with a special emphasis, as if it meant more in her mouth than normal.

'Is that what you want?' I asked bitterly.

'I know how hard it is, but you must try,' she insisted. 'Issy, you have great gifts – gifts of healing, gifts of seeing. But they are trapped in that fire. That's why it comes out all wrong . . . that's why when you touch your power it comes out as harm . . . what you did to Demdyke . . . what you've just done to me today.'

She rolled up her sleeve and showed me how the skin up her arm was bright red; burned.

I stared at the wound and turned away. 'I never will,' I said. 'I never will.' I walked quickly away from the blaze.

Chapter 12

I was angry with her for telling me nothing. I was frightened at what she asked of me. I had been taught all my life to fear fire. I was not sure I wanted to know about myself now, but I still trusted her and loved her. Even when other peculiar things began to happen, I was not at first frightened by them.

I began seeing things out of the corner of my eye. I couldn't see them properly – they might have been animals, or birds or strange little people, but they were never ordinary. I'd catch a glimpse of something, turn my head – and it would be gone. Once, I saw a round green face while I was weeding the cabbages. When I looked again it was nothing – just a fat cabbage plant sitting on the dark earth. A trick of the eyes, I thought; but it had been so clear. Another time I was sitting with my back against the wall of the house, when I saw – or felt – that a long, green arm was leaning out above me. I looked up in alarm – and there was just a runner from the briar rose growing out from the wall over my shoulder.

It was clear to me that Iohan saw these visions too. Once we were planting pea seeds in the garden, spilling them into a little trench we had dug close to the fence. On the other side a big cushion of dark green nettles were pushing against the fence. I had a strange feeling about those nettles and I kept my eye on them. Sure enough, the second Iohan turned away to check on Mark, who was stacking cloth in a little shed behind us, I had a sense of a host of little dark green creatures pushing under the fence and groping through it, a sudden rush of them taking the chance while Iohan was looking the other way. When she turned back she saw me staring.

'Are they trying to get in again?' she growled. She began to poke about next to the fence and grubbed out a handful of roots that had grown under from the nettles on the other side. 'I won't be here much longer, you can have it back then,' she grumbled. The nettles shivered in the breeze. I couldn't help thinking how innocent they looked. 'It's no use looking like that,' snapped Iohan. 'I've got the evidence right here, haven't I?' and she flung the roots at them in a temper.

I often noticed her having words with the weeds that grew around the fence. I've never seen any garden that grew so few weeds as Iohan's.

In another part of the garden was a big elder bush, which was just now coming into its full flush of flower, weeks earlier than similar bushes outside. Once, as I walked past I caught sight of a great golden girl smiling in the sunshine with such a head of pale blonde hair that I stopped in my tracks and stared. And it was nothing but that elder bush, so heavy with flower it was like a great, bright mound of blossom in the grass. A few days later, when Iohan and I were picking the flowers to make syrup, I distinctly heard someone snap angrily at us. I turned round and there was no one there, but as I looked back I caught a glimpse of Iohan plucking a flower from the hair of the golden girl, who was making a face and slapping out at her.

'It's all right, you've get plenty,' said Iohan. 'Why this fuss every year? I never take it all, do I? And I always pay for them.' The golden girl looked sulky for a second, and then there was just the elder bush and Iohan plucking tresses of bright, pale flowers. When she finished, true to her word, she put a mulch of manure around the roots.

I thought it marvellous that her garden should have a life of its own and never thought for a second that these half-seen, half-imagined glimpses of another world might be dangerous. It was only later that I began thinking about imps and devils and then the thought of hell-fire made my scars itch.

The first shadow fell one afternoon about a week after I had arrived. I was in among some bean poles pulling out the dandelions that had crept in and some of them seemed to be trying to get away. I kept catching . . . a glimpse, an idea, I don't know . . . of a little yellow face stealing about behind the beans, tip-toeing, if you can imagine it, and keeping out of sight. I searched and searched, but I couldn't find it and yet I couldn't get rid of the feeling that it was in there somewhere.

At last I got so exasperated I said out loud, 'It's no use hiding, I know you're in there!'

As soon as I said it I realised I was not alone. I looked up. One of Iohan's weavers was standing behind me, and a little to one side was Tolly, who had seen the whole thing. The weaver was staring at me with a look of alarm on his face. He crossed himself rapidly four or five times, muttered something under his breath and hurried off.

I heard what he had called me, and I felt my face turn white. Tolly came over.

'You'd best be careful when there's folk about,' he said. 'They catch glimpses too, and it scares them.' He bent down among the bean poles, rooted about and then grubbed up a fat dandelion plant that was hidden away. 'There he is, see.' He chucked the plant to one side and winked easily at me.

But I couldn't take it like that. That man had called me witch.

'The Bible makes no distinction,' Parson Holden had said. It didn't matter that Iohan was kind and good if her soul was not her own. I remembered Jennet, who was such a dangerous friend to have – poor Jennet, who knew how to love but could not be trusted.

I'd believed witches to be creatures like Demdyke for so long it seemed impossible that

Iohan could be a witch as well. But the more I thought about it, the more dangerous those spirits in the garden seemed to be. For the first time since I had so eagerly set out with her from Pendle that morning, I remembered the things Nat had said about her. 'God will forgive us for accepting her help,' he had said. I was beginning to wish I had never left to come and live with someone familiar with things so unholy.

And then the fire-dream began again. Before I came to Iohan's I had my nightmare only rarely, but she had awakened something in me. I could avoid fire while I was awake, but in my sleep it came back to me.

It happened the night after the weaver had called me witch. It followed the same pattern as ever – the cosy warmth, the sudden snatch out into the blinding light and heat of a blazing fire. But now I knew I was dreaming. My screams parted to let through Iohan's whispering voice . . .

'Look, Issy . . . look . . . Where are you? What do you see?'

'Help me!' I was desperate to find anything that might pull me out of the dream.

'Sssh . . . It's just a dream, nothing's happening. Don't try to wake up. Look around you, Issy. What do you see? Where are you?'

'I can't, I can't,' I moaned. At the same time I felt a surge of rage and bitterness as I realised that far from waking me up, she was trying to keep me in the dream. I began to scream and screech, flinging myself violently from side to side, forcing my head to turn away from the awful unknown sight. I let out a howl of anguish so great that I woke up. I sat up panting. There was Iohan on my bed reaching out to me.

'There's a girl, well done, Issy,' she was saying as she held me to her.

I pushed her away. 'Why didn't you wake me?' I demanded.

She put her arms down and looked sadly at me. 'I told you – you have to see through that fire if you want to know yourself.'

'I don't want to know.'

'I think you do,' she said quietly. 'Anyone can wake you up, but only you can find your way through that dream. It will always come back until you learn to see it through.'

'It's a nightmare, you have to wake me up.'

'Not a nightmare – a memory of when you were small.'

'You know what happened . . . Why can't you just tell me?' I begged.

She shook her head firmly. 'If I tell you, you'll always be imprisoned by it. You have to do it yourself.'

'I don't know . . . I don't want to know!' I felt betrayed and unsafe with her. 'Leave me alone!' I flung myself down on the bed. In a moment she began to move away, but I sat up and begged her to promise she would wake me up if it happened again.

'I can't promise that,' she replied unhappily. 'I can't make any promise that will keep you from yourself.'

'Then I'm going back. You can't keep me here,' I threatened.

There was a pause. 'I'll promise if you make me a promise,' she said at last. 'Promise me that when you feel strong enough, you'll try and see through the fire.'

'I promise,' I said at once. I was certain I would never be so strong.

'Then I promise, too,' said Iohan.

I told myself I should know better than to trust her promises. For the time being she kept her word, but it seemed that Iohan's house was a place for dreams. Three or four times a week I woke from the nightmare with her sitting on my bed shaking me. From time to time she reminded me of my promise, but I always said, 'Not yet.' In fact, I had made up my mind to stay ignorant . . . of the dream, and of my past, if that was to be the cost. I asked Iohan no more questions about myself, or herself. I had begun to distrust her. All my joy in her had gone. I was biding my time until I could go back to Pendle.

Chapter 13

One month after I came to Iohan's house we had visitors. Iohan was counting bales of cloth with me in one of the outhouses when Tolly came and told her that two men were here to see her. I could tell from his look that it was trouble.

They were waiting on their horses outside the house. I recognised them at once. Parson Holden nodded gravely at me as I came into sight. The other one was Bawdwin – the church warden who had been made Witch-finder. He sat stiffly on his horse, holding it tight by the bridle so that it tossed its head irritably. His face was still cold as he watched Iohan walk up to them.

He didn't wait for her to speak. 'We've come for the girl,' he said.

Iohan's eyebrows went up. 'Is that so?' she said.

The man leant over his horse and pointed his finger in her face. He said, 'Witch.'

Iohan glared sullenly at him. I glanced at Parson Holden and he nodded grimly.

'There's a nasty stink about here,' said Iohan. 'Burned flesh and broken bones. The stink of hell.'

'You will be in hell very soon,' he replied, as if he were stating a known fact. 'Mr Priest wishes to save your pupil from the rope. He seems to think her soul is not yet lost. That is not my opinion.'

‘I want to speak to Issy,’ put in Parson Holden. ‘I take it you have no objection?’

Iohan glanced at me. ‘If she wants to. The girl isn’t mine or yours.’

‘Certainly not God’s,’ said the thin man in a jeering voice.

Iohan ignored him. ‘Will you speak with the parson?’ she asked me. I looked at her to see what she wanted and she added, ‘Why not, go ahead. At least he looks as if he’s had some practice smiling.’

Parson Holden dismounted and I led him away to a bench under some fruit trees a little way off. He sat and looked at me grimly before beckoning me to sit by him.

‘How is my father? And Ghyll?’ I asked him, as I sat down.

‘Both in good health,’ he replied. ‘But in very great danger.’

‘What’s happened?’

He peered anxiously into my face. He looked tired and frightened, and I thought: Poor man, all alone in a witch’s house, he must feel terrible.

‘Pendle is all up against the witches,’ he told me. ‘They already have Demdyke, Lizzie and Alizen in jail. God knows what Bawdwin will extract from them. That man’ – he nodded back at the house where we had left Iohan and the Witch-finder – ‘I’ve seen his work. I don’t think the Justice in Lancaster knew what he was doing when he let him loose on Pendle.’ He shook his head miserably. 'Every poor old woman is a witch these days – all it takes is an accusation to be arrested, and once he gets his hands on them . . .' he shrugged.

'Has someone acccused Nat?'

'Not yet. It could happen soon, the way things are.'

'I have to go and see them . . .'

'Issy, you would be certain death to them. You are living with a known witch.' I shook my head but he nodded firmly. 'Iohan a-Style is known for miles around as a witch. Just that she stayed in your father's house might be enough to condemn them – little she cared. As for you, living here – it's madness.'

'I don't believe it.'

He shook his head impatiently. 'For her it's only a matter of time. She's known all over the county, it's an open secret. You can't tell me you've spent three weeks in this house without realising that?'

I looked at the table and shook my head sulkily.

'Issy, listen to me. I've come all this way for your sake. Your only chance is to confess. Tell the truth and I'll do everything I can for you.'

'And what is the truth?' I asked bitterly.

'That you are a witch, that Iohan a-Style is a witch, that Jennet and Demdyke and her family are all witches.'

'Iohan saved Ghyll's life – she saved me from Demdyke. Is that the Devil's work?'

'She has sold her soul. Her powers come from hell. Don't you understand – the Devil doesn't care whether she does good or bad so long as she renounces God and gives him her soul.'

'She told me she doesn't worship the Devil,' I protested.

He grimaced. 'Then she has been deceived,' he said. 'Never forget the cunning of the Devil. There is no lie he will not tell to win a soul. You poor child, you think you've been rescued but you are in worse danger than ever. You must confess – you must testify against her.'

'Would they hang her? And little Jennet, too?'

'They will hang her . . . all of them, Mistress a-Style, Demdyke, little Jennet, fair or foul, young or old, with your help or without it. And they'll hang you too, if you don't do as I say.'

'I can't betray my friends,' I pleaded.

'These creatures you call friends – they're barely human anymore. They have no souls, they're monsters. And you're a witch too, Issy, I'm certain of it. Someone sold your soul when you were too young to remember it – probably this very witch you call your friend. But you were young, you didn't know what you were doing. You haven't abandoned God and He hasn't abandoned you. Remember that – God will never abandon His children, He will forgive everything so long as you truly repent and confess. For you there's still hope. I will testify for you. But you must help me. Do you understand me, Issy? I've come all this way to help you – to try and save your life.'

He had taken hold of my hand and stared

intently at me as he spoke. Now, he turned the hand over to find the mark on my wrist where he had burned me with the candle.

'God forgive me for that,' he murmured, touching the spot gently with his finger. 'This man Bawdwin – he worships the same God as I do, but there's no love in him. If you fall into his hands, God help you. He will have your Iohan before the month's out – even a witch doesn't deserve that.' He sighed unhappily. 'Well, Issy – are you with me? I know it's hard, but it's the only way.'

I thought of all the strange things that had happened since I had met Iohan – the creatures I had seen in the garden, the cures, the way she had cheated Demdyke. I thought of that fire she had shown me. I knew what Parson Holden would make of that, if I told him about it – hell's fire, he'd say. I thought of the mystery of her Thursday nights. Parson Holden was right. Iohan was surely a witch, although a very different one from Demdyke. Very likely so was I. But even the fear of hell was not enough to make me betray her – not yet.

I shook my head.

'Then you are lost,' he said quietly. He kissed my hand and blessed me. 'God save you, Issy,' he said. 'You're a good girl, I know that. But your soul is not your own and you lack the courage to take it back. I'll pray that when the end comes for you it will be quick. If you change your mind . . . my house is always open for you. Remember that.'

He rose and walked back to the house, leaving me sitting on the bench in the sunshine, surrounded by Iohan's flowers.

I'd never felt so miserable. There was no haven for me – even Iohan was turning to poison. There was nowhere for me to turn away from danger.

At the back of my mind I heard the two men speaking to Iohan, and an argument grow up. There was shouting. Iohan let out a yell and then there was a cracking slap, followed by a great thud. I jumped up and rushed over to see what had happened.

Bawdwin was picking himself up out of the dirt with a look of pure venom on his face. Iohan, in a tremendous fury, was coming at him again and she would have kicked his head off if Tolly hadn't run across and pulled her back. Parson Holden helped Bawdwin to his feet.

The side of the man's face was bright red where she had struck him and from the way he scurried away from her boot, she'd already given him the kick of his life.

Iohan shook Tolly off. 'Never speak to any woman like that again,' she hissed. Her face was livid with anger. 'Where do you get your filthy poison from? Not God surely.'

The Witch-finder limped over to his horse and crawled up it. It was a great big animal with muddy frills of hair around its huge feet and wide high shoulders. Once he was up above, Bawdwin found his courage again.

'You'll pay for that,' he spat, wiping the mud off his face. He looked like a small angry bird, perched up there on the great beast. Iohan glared up at him as he pulled at the reins and trotted a few metres down the track. But then he turned and said suddenly,

'Show me your hands, witch.'

I felt her quiver by my side and I turned to look at her. It was the only time I ever saw Iohan at a loss for words. She had lifted her hands up as if they were not part of her but some precious possession and held them loosely below her thoat. She had turned grey. Her lips moved, but no words came out.

The thin man nodded with a hard little smile of pleasure. 'The witch remembers,' he said. 'When you come before me I shall remember this.'

I noticed Holden looking at him with an expression of disgust as he turned his horse again. They were both trotting off down the track when Iohan suddenly found her voice.

'I remember what they did to the hands of Jesus Christ,' she said.

The Witch-finder dragged his horse round and snarled at her. 'Do you compare yourself to our Lord, witch?'

'No,' she answered. 'I compare you to His murderers.'

The thin man went white. I held my breath at her nerve. His mouth became a thin knife slash in his face and he fought to control himself before he was able to answer, 'It's God's work.'

'God's work?' she jeered. 'Where in the Gospel does our Lord tear the living flesh off his enemies? You have been deceived. But you will answer for your crimes against nature, in hell.'

To be threatened by a witch with hell was too much. He swore and dragged the horse round to face her so violently that he tore its mouth with the bit. Frightened and bleeding, the animal reared, slashed at the air and tried to turn from her. But he wrenched it back and drove in his spurs. The horse whinnied, pranced, cut the air with its hooves once more and then suddenly bounded forward directly at Iohan. The thin man lifted his whip. Iohan, tiny and frail under those huge hooves, raised her arm to her face . . .

'Don't!' I heard myself shout. I ran forward. Somewhere at the back of my head I heard the roar and blaze of fire. I felt the power flow into me in a smooth sudden movement so wide and broad that it filled me up in a second and then paused, waiting for the moment of release. I lifted my arms and pushed them forward towards the horse and the fire leapt from my fingers, rushed out of me in one great surge, a wave of power. For a second I saw horse and rider caught in the inferno, blazing and screaming. There was a smell of burnt hair. Then the fire lifted them right into the air, like a branch of wood going over a wave. The horse found itself suddenly up on its hind legs. It pranced, tried to jump forward but could not, hung for a second on tip-toes and then tumbled and fell backwards into the dirt. It crashed right into a bed of marigolds by the side of the track and began thrashing and whinneying, kicking clods of earth everywhere as it tried to regain its feet. The fire stopped. There was a blue haze in the air. The whole thing had taken just a few seconds.

I thought for a second it had been a dream. But there was the horse struggling to its feet; there was the Witch-finder rolling over on his back among the flowers to avoid being crushed. The smell of singed hair was still in the air, and I saw how the skin on his face had turned a bright, angry red. The horse clambered up on its feet and fled off down the yard, its mane smouldering. The man picked himself up for the second time, his eyes fixed on me, his face grey with fear, blotched red with burns. I took a step towards him and he backed away screaming at me and crossing himself. Parson Holden came up from behind and snatched him into his saddle. As they galloped off I could see the thin man's face staring backwards at me.

'Witch, witch!' he screamed in a high, boy's voice. Then the horse swerved before the fence, steadied, jumped and cleared it. They disappeared behind the trees lining the road beyond our land.

As the drumming of the horses' hooves disappeared, everything went very quiet. I saw Iohan looking at me and Tolly, who shook his head and glanced up and down the road to see if anyone was watching. Iohan laughed with delight, seized my hand and dragged me after her into the house.

Chapter 14

I was saying, 'I couldn't help it, I couldn't help it,' over and over again. Iohan sat me down and gave me something to drink and there must have been something in it, because I stopped shaking almost at once. She looked into my face and nodded, and then flopped down next to me in a chair.

'Issy girl,' she said, 'if you ever lose your temper with me, let me know so that I can get well away.' Then she giggled. 'Did you see his face when he was flying backwards? I thought you were going to knock him all the way back to Pendle. And the horse! I've never seen an animal look so surprised.' She began to laugh, but when she looked across to me and saw my face she stopped.

'I couldn't help it, it just happened,' I told her.

'You have great gifts. You have to learn to control them.'

'I didn't do anything,' I insisted.

'You saved my life.'

'It wasn't me, the horse just fell, he must have overbalanced – he was frightened, wasn't he?' I babbled. But it was no use. I couldn't even convince myself.

'I saw the fire – the dream fire,' I said. 'It was there the whole time.'

Iohan nodded. 'That fire is the key to your strength,' she told me. 'It stands between you and the talents God has given you.'

'Then it's true, isn't it . . . I am a witch just like they say.'

Iohan scoffed. 'What's a witch? Someone who digs up dead people and makes ointment out of babies and curses honest neighbours for not doing as they're told? You don't do any of those things, do you?'

'But I can do things . . . And you . . . he said that you're a witch . . . he said everyone knows it.'

'Do you think I'm a witch?'

I cried, 'I don't know.'

'What makes a witch? Tell me that.'

I knew the answer to that one. 'Someone who has sold their soul to the Devil.'

'I can promise you that I'm not one of them, and never have been and never will be . . . and neither are you, no matter what ignorant people say. I have nothing to do with the Devil and I have nothing to do with harm.'

'But those things I saw in your garden – what are they? And what did I do just then – I don't understand,' I begged. 'What does the fire mean? And what did he mean about your hands?'

When I mentioned her hands, Iohan lifted them up and cradled them on her breast, as if she were holding a little bird or some other delicate thing. When I reached out and took one of them in mine she flinched but didn't stop me. I took off the loose woollen under-glove that she always wore.

There were little ridges and bumps all along the bones of her fingers, and I realised they had once been broken, each finger many times. There was something else that was odd and it took a moment to notice. Iohan had no fingernails.

'Poor Iohan,' I said. Without thinking I lifted the hand and kissed it.

'I was accused of witchcraft once before,' she said. Her voice seemed to have gone tiny and thin, like a frightened little girl.

I carefully placed the hand back in her lap and she put her glove back on.

'If you ever fall into their hands,' she said in the same little voice, 'remember what I tell you now . . . you must confess to whatever they ask you . . . about yourself, about me, about Nat, about Ghyll, about anyone and anything. No one is loyal in the torture chamber. All you can hope for is to be lucky and win a quick death.'

'You didn't confess, though,' I said.

She smiled thinly. 'I confessed,' she said.

Iohan refused to tell me anymore about what had happened to her – or me – in Scotland when I was still a baby. But that evening, Tolly came round to eat our evening meal with us and they told me about themselves and what they were.

She was a witch, after all she had said. She insisted that it was different with her – 'not like Demdyke's brood'. Demdyke and her kind were debased witches, witches who had forgotten why there were here, what they were for and even who they worshipped. The true god of the witches was not the Devil, she said, and he had nothing to do with evil.

I remembered the words of Parson Holden – 'Never forget the cunning of the Devil . . .' I must have looked doubtful, because she sighed and shook her head.

'He's not like that, they just want to make an enemy out of him. Doesn't the Christian God say Himself that He is a jealous God? Our god has no arguments with anyone; he simply is what he is. He's not just the god of men and women, but the god of the fields and the trees and the birds and the animals – of all living things. All things worship him. He is the god of life and death. Now, only the beasts and the plants still know him – people have forgotten. There are so few of us left – most of the witches are like Demdyke. When there is no one left to remember him, then mankind will have lost all touch with nature and they will begin to destroy the world.'

The god had once been worshipped all over Europe, she told me. First the pagan gods had pushed him to one side and then when the Christians came they tried to turn him into their Devil and discredit him and make an enemy of him. Demdyke and her like had come to believe these lies. Now they thought that they worshipped the maker of evil.

That was why I saw those faces and shapes in

the garden – because this was a place where the spirits were not just of people, but of plants and animals which came alive for those who could see. As for those Thursday nights, it was the Sabbat they went to, but not the Sabbat of Demdyke, with waxen images and curses.

'Dancing. Singing. We have a party,' smiled Tolly. 'You'll see for yourself one day.'

It was clear that they regarded me as one of them. I had the same gifts they had – the gifts of their god, gifts of healing, of harming, of seeing.

'There's no good or bad in it,' explained Iohan. 'Just as you can lead a good life or a bad life, you can use your power for good or for bad. Demdyke chose the bad – we, the good. I hope you will, too.'

I went to bed with a great deal on my mind that night. Someone was deceived. Was it Parson Holden or Iohan? I had no way of knowing.

Chapter 15

Once before Iohan had had to leave her home and flee. Now the time had come again. Things had been getting dangerous for some time and with the arrival of Bawdwin and what I had done to him, the danger was very close.

Tolly wanted to shut up shop and disappear overnight, but Iohan was too much the business woman to do that. If she left now she would leave a great deal of her money tied up, not to mention leaving many of her weavers with pieces of cloth they had no way of selling. She only needed a couple more weeks to close the business down.

Tolly looked grim and shook his head, but she would not be moved. 'They still have no evidence,' she argued. 'What's he to say – that a twelve-year-old girl picked up his horse and flung him down on his backside?' She gurgled delightedly at the thought of Bawdwin admitting to that indignity. 'He'll not get a warrant like that!'

As for me, I was filled with a sense of danger closing in around me, but from where did the danger come? From Bawdwin of course – but I did not forget what I had been taught all my life about witches and hell-fire. Parson Holden would never help me after what I had done. To go back to Pendle was suicide for me and deadly to Nat and Ghyll. There was nowhere for me.

*

At last something happened that brought the whole matter to a head. It began with a little thing, a silly thing that for some reason frightened me where everything else had not really mattered. It was a Monday afternoon, just a week before the pack horses were due to leave. Since we had decided to abandon the house we let the garden run wild. The weeds lost no time in jumping over the fence and getting rooted in the rich, cultivated soil.

Now that Iohan no longer forbade them they were really making up for lost time, and by the end of a week the whole garden was covered with a carpet of tiny dandelions, shepherd's purse and forget-me-nots, about a centimetre high. The weeds got terribly excited and it became a very odd experience just walking up the garden path. Things were going on everywhere. You felt that the garden was so infested, it wanted to jump up and give itself a good shake.

On this particular afternoon, I was wandering about when I heard a strange sound coming from behind one of the little sheds littered around the garden. I crept I up to it and peered round.

There was one of Iohan's cats sitting in the sun on the wooden steps leading up to the shed door. It was crying.

The poor thing must have been crying for some time, because there were splashes of wet on the wood between its paws and the fur on its face was soaked. It kept licking its face and trying to wipe the tears away with its paws, but it wasn't getting very far with it. Its mews were coming out all wrong, mixed up with tears and sobs and little cries, and it kept shaking its head and moaning and rubbing its eyes, but it just couldn't stop.

I stood and stared for maybe a minute until I made a little noise and the cat looked up and saw me. It jumped up in surprise and ran down the steps behind the shed. I peered round after it just in time to see it throw me a piercing glance before it disappeared into the house. I had the strange impression it was going to tell Iohan what had happened.

Straight away I thought of Demdyke's imp, Tibb. *Cats don't cry,* I thought. The things in the garden had been impressions in the shadows, half seen, half imagined. But this was real; and *cats don't cry*. Later on, Iohan said that she had taken its kittens away to be drowned. Since we were all leaving and there would be no one to look after them, it seemed the kindest thing to do.

'You see how it is with us,' she added. 'We help things to know what they are – to know themselves – the cat as well as you. She lost her kittens and she's sad about it. Why shouldn't she be sad?'

I couldn't speak to them properly after that. I found myself avoiding their company. Once, when Iohan tried to touch me I shrank away without meaning to. She looked queerly at me and asked what was wrong, but I just shrugged and left before she could press me. Fortunately both she and Tolly were so busy I was able to keep myself to myself until bedtime.

Cats don't cry. I had stopped trusting her. *Cats don't cry.* I no longer knew if she was good or bad.

There was one way to get at the truth. In two days' time was the Sabbat. I would go along and see for myself.

As usual we had supper early on Thursday night. This was the high spot of Iohan's week and as soon as the meal was over, she disappeared into one of her little sheds to get herself ready. Tolly vanished too, to get ready in his way. This was the first time they had made no secret of what they were doing, and I was curious to see how they prepared themselves.

Tolly managed to slip away early, so I never saw him ready for the service. When Iohan came out she was brushed and washed and moist-eyed with excitement. She had her hair tied up behind and was wearing a black linen robe with a hood – black, to help her hide in the dark if she had to, she claimed. Despite the colour, she reminded me of nothing so much as a bride. She had a little silver brooch shaped like a horned moon and asked me to help fix it on her breast. She was chattering away like a girl the whole time about how much she was looking forward to it, and how glorious it was, and what fun they had and how much better it was in every way than the dull, lecturing church services. And she kept giggling and laughing that wonderful gurgling laugh of hers as if it was the best fun in the world.

'You'll see for yourself one day,' she promised as she kissed me goodbye by the gate. 'Can't you feel it? Even the trees and the fields are excited because they know that he is coming. Tonight, the moss and seeds and buds know that they are loved and needed and have a place on earth specially their own. I know you'll love him, Issy, when you see him for yourself.' She stroked my cheek, kissed me and then ran off into the darkness under the trees. I waited a few seconds, and followed quietly behind her.

It was a dark April night, still, cold and damp. There was a sliver of a moon, very high and white, floating like a bowl above the trees. It shed little light and I could barely make out Iohan as she moved quickly and quietly among the trees and bushes beyond the garden.

Her way led her through the fields behind our house and up the valley to the moor above us. Up there, where the sky was open, she became easier to follow as I could see her outlined against the sky. We travelled a mile or more before we began to descend and I heard voices. Another figure passed close by me. I lay down in the grass to let them pass. There were more voices and a few minutes later flames flickered in a hollow below.

Figures were gathering around the fire. I saw Iohan throw off her hood. Here was the Sabbat.

The witches came to the fire out of the darkness. I recognised several of Iohan's neighbours and customers among them. Maybe a dozen or so milled around the fire. Then there was a drum and the whine of some pipe music and the worshippers began to dance.

It was like no religious service I had ever seen. There were no words, just the excited rhythms of the music whipping across the moor and the robed dancers moving around the fire, moving in and out of each other's arms. There was laughter and shouting as they whirled faster and faster. I could imagine what Parson Holden would make of this worship, although it seemed all in good spirits – like a party or a festival rather than a service.

The dancers stamped, clapped their hands, shouted in time to the music. They began to whirl and dance with a fierce energy. More drums joined in. The pace grew hotter and louder and faster until the air was full of noise – of shouting, of drumbeats, of clapping, stamping, whooping people; and at that moment there stepped from behind the fire a horned figure.

The world turned red in front of my eyes. It was all lies, she was nothing but lies. This was her god, this was the one she ran to like a girl bride. I felt the jabbing pain of that candle end Parson Holden had pushed against my wrist and the words – 'Hell-fire . . . this is what it feels like forever and ever and ever and ever . . .'

I began to shake and my hands came up to my face. I told myself, 'Don't look, don't look, he will know, he will see you – it's a sin even to look at him . . .' but I couldn't drag my eyes away.

The witches' chorus rose into a shrieking crescendo. I saw Iohan, her face flushed, her mouth wide open as she beat her hands together. The Horned Man lifted his arms as they cried out to him, and then rushed in among them, dashing at them with his horns, spinning on his heels, roaring like a bull. They screamed and yelled and danced furiously around him, taunting him to come and touch them with his great horns. They ran up to embrace him or kiss his shoulder or his back, stroke him, love him . . . and then at last I saw Iohan jump up on his back and plant a kiss at the base of his pale horn where it sprouted from his temple . . .

I screamed. The scream came from my soul and I could never have stopped it. There was so much noise, but someone heard me. I saw them turn and look up. The music faltered. I was still standing. He turned, his deformed head sweeping those great horns round and I saw his arm lift to point at me. He knew me, he had me, I was his forever in hell . . .

This was the one Iohan told me I should come to love. There was no mistaking the Devil.

Chapter 16

All I wanted was to give myself up, to give anyone up – Iohan, Jennet, Nat, anyone – just so long as I could leave that figure behind. I ran and ran, tripping and falling and bruising myself and telling myself over and over, 'You can't run from the Devil, you can't run from the Devil . . .' and at last my breath gave out and I couldn't run another step. I fell over for a last time and lay there in the grass, waiting for those horns to loom across the dark sky and for that blunt, ugly head to turn towards me . . .

I was so certain he would come that I waited there even after my breath had returned and I could hear the stillness of the night around me. Gradually I grew cold. I had been lying on the damp grass for perhaps twenty minutes. I was convinced that he was just over the edge of the grass and that the second I lifted my head I would see him sitting next to me, waiting. But at last I couldn't stay still anymore and I raised myself.

Clouds had thickened over the moon and stars. I couldn't see more than three or four metres around me. The darkness was his. Of course, he was all around me. I crossed myself and prayed that the half animal shape of him could not come outside the little temple his worshippers had made for him. I began to run again.

If I'd had the strength I would have run straight across the moors to Pendle and Parson Holden in one stretch. You can't run from the Devil; but perhaps it was possible to hide from his servants, the witches. The way towards Pendle lay past Iohan's house, and I had enough sense to dash in and snatch a few things for the journey – a hunk of bread, some cheese and my money that I had hidden in a cloth by my bedside. Then I continued my flight.

As I ran I prayed under my breath, begging God to forgive me . . . I'm sorry, God, I'm sorry, begging Him to keep me from harm, begging Him to take me back from the enemy. Now I understood how cunning the Devil was, just as Parson Holden has said, how he twisted and lied and entered right into your mind and heart until you no longer knew good from bad, right from wrong. I promised never again to doubt what a witch really was, to deny such thoughts a home in me, to refuse even to think them. I had been a vessel for the Devil's power. I had sinned so much I was unfit to live. It would be better for everyone if I were hanged.

It took me half an hour to reach the pack-horse track. Although the weather had been dry lately the passage of the horses through the long winter had made such a broken, sticky bog of the road that it was impossible on foot. I tried to run on the turf alongside, but even that was so riven with potholes I could barely walk, let alone run in that dark night. I staggered and clawed my way along the ground. Every step was blind. I was quickly exhausted but I forced myself forward. At last I came to a barn by the roadside and decided I would be better to save my strength for when it was light.

Inside there was straw to cover me, but I was too frightened to sleep. Every rustle in the grass outside, every creak of the old beams was some imp or sprite and the old owl who hunted mice in the dark was the Devil's eye. Then it occurred to me that surely witches, too, could see in the night; they would follow me and look in the barn. I was mad to be here. I crept out and tried to lie down in the grass some way off the track, but the damp and the wind chilled me. I moved again and lay by the barn wall wrapped in straw. It was not so cold but I still couldn't sleep. I was alone in the Devil's land while the creatures of night, all his things, watched and marked me for their master. Finally, I preferred exhaustion to this miserable waiting and I rose in the darkness to continue.

Even when the light came it was no help. I tried to run faster but I just fell all the more. Then I realised . . . of course . . . it had been some trick of his to make me lie down in the grass and wait for them. He lived in my own mind. Did I think they would be lying freezing in the grass because it was dark? How had I been so foolish – I had lost hours with my stupidity.

I was so mad with fright I even believed the

ground beneath me was on his side, the way it tore and clawed me off my feet. And all the time I thought: they will know what has happened . . . they will know which way I've gone . . . they will walk faster than I . . . they will have horses . . . their master will help them. I prayed as I ran, but I did not believe.

At last, an hour after sunrise, I thought my prayers had been answered. I heard ahead of me the jangle of the rumbler bells carried across on the wind. There was a pack-horse train ahead of me. I pushed on. Soon, I could even hear the squelch of the great hooves in the sticky mud, and I thought, as soon as I get over the rise I'll see them.

I trudged on, expecting to see the round high packs of the horses rolling over every rise, but I forgot how sound carries across the open moor and when I turned the top of the hill and saw the team lumbering ahead maybe half a mile away, I could have wept. At least it was downhill now. I ran through the reedy grass, tripping and stumbling in the mud and glancing over my shoulder, expecting to see the Devil himself riding over the tops after me. At last I was near enough to shout to the man at the end of the team.

I tried to tell him my problem, but I was so out of breath I could hardly speak. In the end he put me atop the shambling horse by his side and told me to catch my breath.

When I mentioned witches he frowned and for

a second I thought that he was one himself. But it was not that that scared him.

'I can't put my team to the risk of witches for the sake of a girl. You'll have to get down.'

I begged him, but he was adamant. I was sick. For all my desperation I had come just a few miles from Iohan's house. If he put me down I was lost. In the end, I remembered the silver coins – Iohan's coins, likely the Devil's money. But I had no choice.

The man stared at the sight of silver, took it, bit it and grinned up at me. 'My livelihood is safe, at least,' he said. 'The closest we're going to Colne is Marsden. I'll take you there, but you'll have to get down outside the town.'

I nodded; anything, anywhere would have done me.

The stubby Galloway horses were carrying coal on their backs across the moors. The man laid blankets atop the pack and I was able to stretch out without any fear of tumbling off. He hid me under another blanket so I couldn't be seen perched high up on the tall pack. It was as comfortable as a feather bed to me at that moment. I was exhausted after my ordeal; the horse's rolling walk carried me away from the witches, away from Iohan, the Devil and all. Before I knew it I fell asleep, rocked away across the moors, like a baby in a great, warm cradle.

I was woken some time later by the sound of light

rain pattering on my cloak. I felt calm and clear again and the terrors of the night before seemed less urgent. I poked my head out from under the blanket and asked where we were.

'Just coming down to Marsden,' the man replied. 'You've been asleep four hours, girly,' he added with a smile.

'And no one's come for me?' I asked.

'They came all right. Man on a bay horse rode up and wanted to know if I'd seen a girl your age. He gave a good description of you – said you were a maidservant run off after having stole your master's money.'

He looked up questioningly at me. I shook my head.

He shrugged. 'It don't matter to me if you're a saint, a witch, a beggar, a queen or a thief – so long as I have your silver in my pocket,' he said cheerfully. 'Anyhow, I told him I'd passed such a girl way back before the Pack Horse Inn, so I expect he's digging about round there now. No, don't thank me, you paid me for it. Get back under the blanket now, I don't want my mates up ahead to see what I've got on board. They'd want paying too. Here – I expect you're hungry.' He handed me up some water in a flask and a hunk of bread and waved me back away out of sight under the blanket.

I put the bread in my pocket till later, but drank some water. As we rocked down into the village of Marsden, I thought how money made even villains into the nicest of men.

As the dusk began to gather, the horses stopped to make camp for the night. I heard the men shouting to one another and shortly after my helper got me down and pointed me along a valley.

'There's your way to Colne,' he told me. 'There's a barn just half a mile along the valley, with plenty of straw – it'll be a warm and dry place to get some sleep.'

I thanked him and ran off into the valley before his friends spotted me. As I walked the air got colder and the light failed and I decided to take his advice and bed down in the barn.

Alone again in the dark, some of my old fears returned. But I was still exhausted and soon fell asleep. When I woke the sun was up, it was a bright, clear, cold day. In another few hours I would be safely under lock and key.

Chapter 17

As I walked along the valley I could see the hulk of Pendle Hill. Across there were the little houses of the Roughlee, my old home. It was like another world now. I would have loved to call and see Nat and Ghyll, but it was too dangerous for them. I turned my face away and carried on towards Colne, draped across the hillsides in front of me.

But as I drew near my goal, the Devil whispered to me again and my will began to slacken. It was one thing to confess myself, but I knew that would not be enough. They would want me to accuse Iohan and Tolly. And now that seemed hard. I thought of Iohan's hands. I forgot about the Horned Man and instead saw Iohan laughing with fun. I saw the friendly spirits in her garden. I thought of serious old Tolly tucking the baby cabbages in the earth as if he were putting them to bed, and when I thought that I had to bring them to jail and cause them to be broken and whipped and hanged, I did not feel holy about it. It made me sick.

I told myself, 'It is the Devil speaking to you, don't listen.' I remembered my promise not to think such thoughts again. But my doubts were too strong to be ignored. For the first time in ages I thought of Jennet, and suddenly I wanted to see her. There was no difference between us now, we were both witches against our will. I thought bitterly, foul witch that I was, I could not keep away from my own kind, not even when I could put my soul out of danger within the hour.

But then I thought I could do some good in my last hours of freedom. Perhaps I could convince Jennet to come with me to confess. That would help redeem my soul and perhaps save her as well. Parson Holden had told me that if I confessed I might not be hanged – why not Jennet too? That provided me with an excuse. I turned my face away from Colne and headed up towards Pendle and Malkin Tower.

The sun was shedding some early warmth on the pastures under Pendle Hill. I thought it unlikely that the witches would be at home when the weather was good and when I first got there it seemed that there was no one home. Even so, I was too scared to go near and hid behind a wall some way off to wait for Jennet.

A few minutes later Jennet came out of the hovel followed by her Uncle James. They were filthier than ever and they moved slowly out into the thin sunshine, like a pair of big, damaged insects, picking their way with careful little steps over the rubbish around the hovel.

James crept round out of the wind and sat with his back to the wall, huddling himself up and pulling his rags closely around him. He seemed to be very tired, but I saw his bright, intense gaze at the dirt between his knees before he closed his eyes and hung his head. I thought he must be suffering in some way.

Jennet followed him and sat a few metres off. She was wearing even less than he was, and she just folded her arms around her little chest, let her head loll to one side and stared listlessly away beyond the hills towards Colne.

The two sat not speaking for several minutes. Eventually James spoke. Jennet shook her head. He got angry and shouted, and she climbed up onto her feet and began to loiter off down the hill towards Colne. Again, that strange, picking, cautious walk.

I waited until she was out of sight of the house and then ran to catch her up. She heard my feet on the ground and turned. She took a couple of steps towards me, but then stopped.

I thought at first that she must not be pleased to see me from the way she just stood there, but when I got to her she clung on to me and whispered my name in my hair over and over, and began to cry. As I squeezed her back, I knew why she hadn't run to me and why she walked like an old woman. Every bone on her body stuck out like knuckles through her dry skin. She leaned against me as if the effort to stand was too much. She and James were starving to death.

We stood for a minute like that in the middle of the stony field, embracing in the wind. Then Jennet muttered, 'Let's get into some shelter.' She nodded to a shepherd's hut in the next field. We made our way over the stony pasture towards it.

'No one gives us anything these past few weeks,' she said.

I had given Jennet the remains of the bread in my pack. She had been without food for so long she seemed to have forgotten hunger and began gnawing at it tiredly, but as she ate her hunger returned, and she finished by bolting it down like a dog. Then she lay back to digest it. She saw me looking at her fleshless thighs and grimaced. 'They've decided to wipe us out,' she told me.

Bawdwin's word was law in Pendle now. No one dared give food to the witches for fear of being accused themselves. There were always people glad of an excuse to turn their backs on the beggars, witches or not, but now even the more generous folk had a chance to take their revenge for the years of fear Demdyke and her family had held over them. Then, a few weeks ago, Alizen had met a packman on her way into Colne and tried to beg pins from him. He had refused and she had cursed him. Not a mile later, he had fallen to the ground paralysed and unable to speak.

Everyone was surprised, not least Alizen, and Demdyke believed it must surely be nothing more than coincidence. But Alizen was convinced she had done it and was conscience-stricken.

This was the chance the Witch-finder had been waiting for. He had interviewed Alizen and got a confession from her. On the strength of it he had arrested Demdyke and Lizzie. The rumour was they had been tortured, and now every witch in Pendle lived in fear of arrest.

It was not just the witches who lived in fear. Once you had fallen into Bawdwin's hands, it made little difference whether you were a witch or not. You would certainly confess to whatever lies he put into your mouth.

With the feared old women put away, all hold the Malkin Tower brood held over the poor people melted away. They had become outcasts and barely a crust or a penny had been given them since that time. Only Nat had helped them, although he had little enough to spare. Since the coming of the Witch-finder he had made no business himself as a cunning man and had to accept help from his neighbours. Now, even he gave nothing. Parson Holden had ordered him to cease under threat of arrest.

I was glad to hear that Nat and Ghyll were safe and well. It had happened in the past that wisemen had to lie low once in a while, and I knew he had good neighbours who would help him until good times came again. But the witches had no such friends and it was a miserable fate to be starved to death in the middle of the community that bred them. Jennet told me it was only a matter of time before she and James were arrested. She actually looked forward to it, as at least in jail she would get something to eat, however poor.

When I told Jennet my story she nodded.

'Grandmother said that Iohan a-Style must be a powerful witch to trick her like that.' She giggled. 'She was very angry. When she went round to show Ghyll the real mannikin, he laughed at her and she couldn't do anything about it.'

When I told her how I had seen the Devil at the Sabbat, her eyes went wide.

'Then she must be very powerful,' she said. 'At our Sabbat we only ever have a man who dresses up.'

And suddenly, I doubted everything all over again. It had all been such a long way off – it was night, I was frightened. Could it have been only that – a man in a mask? I told myself that again the Devil was worming his way back into me, that I was filthy with sin, that I had to fight those seeds of doubt. I hurried on to tell her about my plan.

'We can confess together,' I urged her. 'Perhaps it will save you as well.'

Jennet shivered. 'They'll hang me,' she whimpered.

'Perhaps – but at least your soul will be safe.'

'I sold my soul,' she whispered. 'I showed you the mark. I belong to him, now.'

There was no need between us to ask who 'he' was.

I told Jennet what Parson Holden had told me – that God never abandoned His children, that He would forgive us everything so long as we truly repented and confessed. This seemed to be a new idea to her. She said that Demdyke had told her that once she had sold her soul it was gone for good, and nothing and no one could ever get it back for her.

'That's what the Devil wants you to believe,' I told her. 'He doesn't want you to know that God is still waiting for you. Parson Holden said. He said that he might even be able to save me from the gallows. You don't think he'd lie, do you?'

Jennet thought not. 'And I have to confess to being a witch . . . and to Grandmother and Mother and Uncle James?' she asked.

I hesitated. But that was what the parson had said, and I nodded.

Jennet took my hand. 'Did the parson really say it? Did he really say it? I can stop being a witch if I confess?'

'Yes, he said that.'

'Then I'll do it. I hate them. They made me a witch, I never wanted to – you know that. You'll tell them, won't you.'

'Yes, I'll tell them.'

'Are we going to do it now?'

'Yes, now,' I told her. She took my hand and we trailed down the hill, towards Colne.

Chapter 18

Now that Jennet had made up her mind, she was filled with a fierce joy at betraying her family. They had tormented and bullied her all her life, but now she was to be free of them and to have them in her power for once.

I trailed miserably after her. It was not for this that the parson had asked – not for hatred and revenge, but for a kind of ruthless honesty. I couldn't find a way to explain it and as Jennet chattered away and we drew nearer again to Colne, my heart grew blacker and darker and more miserable. I could see nothing honest in myself, either. I asked Jennet about Iohan's story that the witches' god was not the Devil at all, but someone older than the Christian God, a god of animals and of the fields.

Yes, she had heard that story. Some of the other witches had told her that even though he had horns like the Devil, that was a sign only that he was Lord of the Beasts as well as Lord of Men. They said that old Demdyke had forgotten who he was and come to believe all the Christian stories about Satan and Devil worship. These witches wanted to help and not to harm and claimed that their god was more like the Christian God than the Devil. But Demdyke scoffed at them and said they were fooling themselves and that it would be worse for them in hell if they did not do harm as their master wished them to.

What was false, what was good, what was bad? I had no idea where to start. Jennet held me tightly by the hand and pulled me into Colne town to confess to the Christian priest and turn our own people over to the gallows.

We never made it. When we reached Colne it became clear that everything was already up with us. We came out onto a track with some scattered wooden houses by it leading into the main part of the town. We were only a little way up the road when we were recognised.

'There's the little witch!' someone shouted. People ran up to see us and soon we were surrounded by a crowd, men and women and children, young and old, hooting and shouting angrily at us.

'You're going to hang, Jennet Demdyke,' someone shouted. A cry of approval went up. Someone threw a stone that struck her arm, and it must have hurt her terribly because she cried out and nearly fell. She had so little flesh. But she pulled herself up and pushed forward, trying not to show it.

'We're going to confess and get back our souls,' she shouted. 'I'll be as good as any of you.'

That shut some of them up, but one shouted out, 'It's too late to confess now, you little witch – they're out hunting you down this minute!'

'She's trying to get out of it, now she knows it's all up,' cried another.

This angered the crowd further and they pushed closer to us.

'And that other one's a witch too – she's the one they say burned Bawdwin . . .' They backed off when they heard that. It seemed I was famous in my own town. But by now the street was packed with people and we had to struggle against them to move up the road. We were only two small girls, pushed and shoved by grown men and women, and they soon discovered we couldn't harm them. Finally a group of men decided confession was too good for us. They seized us and dragged us up a lane away from the parsonage towards the magistrate's house.

The crowd was getting bigger all the time, very angry and excited. I thought they would kill us. We were lifted up into the air and carried along on a flood of screaming people, punching and poking at us as we passed overhead. Then we were thrown down onto the cobbles and kicked up to the magistrate's door. Some big brute stood over us, bellowing, 'Here's two more witches for the gallows!' and kicked viciously at our legs. Then the door opened and a footman dragged us inside.

The lackey who pulled us in was not an unkind man. He gave us some milk and oat cakes, and checked to make sure we had no bones broken. But when he handed us over to the jailer we had no doubt we were prisoners. He took us down underground, along a passage and past a number of heavy doors. He unlocked one of these and motioned us to enter.

Inside was a low cellar, too low to stand upright in. The floor was damp mud. There was nothing to sit or lie on. All we had for a toilet was a bucket in a corner.

The magistrate was out with Bawdwin. He came back late and ate. We stayed down there for about five hours before we were summoned up to confess. There were three men waiting for us. Magistrate Nowell had Parson Holden with him, and I was grateful for that. But on his other side was Bawdwin, the Witch-finder. His face was still scarred by bright red streaks, and his mouth hardened when I came in.

'That's her, the worst of them,' he hissed when he saw me.

Jennet glanced at me. 'We were coming to confess,' she said in a shrill voice.

'They were on their way to the parsonage when the crowd took them,' agreed Parson Holden, but Bawdwin shook his head.

'No witch ever confessed without persuasion,' he said. I knew what sort of persuasion he had in mind.

Jennet seized my arm. 'Issy told me that if I confessed myself and my family, God would take my soul back from the Devil.' I saw all their eyebrows go up at this remark, but Jennet went on, 'I never wanted it . . . they made me do it . . . Demdyke and the rest. They said that once the Devil had my soul I'd never be able to get it back, but if they were lying, I'd like very much to get it back.' She appealed to Parson Holden. 'She said you told her, sir, and you wouldn't tell Issy a lie, would you, sir?'

Holden nodded, and the magistrate agreed. 'If you truly repent God will forgive you,' he said.

'Do you really want to live a Christian life, Jennet?' asked Holden earnestly. Jennet nodded fervently. 'And are you willing to tell us everything we want to know?' he asked.

'Everything, against them. I don't owe them anything,' swore Jennet.

The parson nodded. 'Then there's no reason why you shouldn't lead a long and a useful Christian life,' he said, glancing at the magistrate, who in turn glanced at the Witch-finder, but nodded in agreement.

'God will certainly forgive you . . . He has promised that. As for the Justice . . . we will do all we can for you if you confess fully.'

Bawdwin twisted irritably in his chair.

'"Thou shalt not suffer a witch to live,"' he snapped. 'It's not for man to forgive her, she must be sent to her Maker for judgement. Why take her word for it when I can squeeze all we need to know out of her? Leave her with me for an hour and I'll tell you everything she knows.'

Nowell looked coldly at him. 'I've seen enough

of your work,' he growled. 'Besides, we need some voluntary information. The judge at Lancaster might well not accept information if you have to break bones to get at it.'

Bawdwin curled his lip, and I gathered that he thought the Lancaster judge a tougher man than Nowell made out. But the magistrate had his way. He called in a clerk to take down Jennet's words, and she began to talk.

She accused everyone – her mother, her grandmother, her sister, her uncle. There had been a meeting of witches at Malkin Tower after Demdyke's arrest, and Jennet reeled off the names of twenty-odd of her neighbours. She named their imps and told their plots, when they had met, where they met, what they had said and done, whom they had bewitched and whom they had murdered. The clerk scribbled away, trying to keep up with her. Occasionally one of the three men would ask her a question. Jennet's voice piped on and on. I wondered how many good people like Iohan and Tolly, as well as the Demdykes, would end their lives choking on a rope, or rotting in a wet dungeon, or crying out at the hands of the Witch-finder, because of that half hour of frightened jabber. The three men smiled. Even Parson Holden was pleased with the night's work.

At last Nowell nodded. 'We have enough to hammer them all,' he said. Now he looked at me.

'It's your turn, Issy,' said Holden. 'The same is true for you . . .' But Bawdwin rose to his feet.

'You saw what she did,' he hissed.

'The same applies to Isabel,' went on Holden firmly. 'The child has committed no crime that carries the death penalty.'

The Witch-finder's face turned so white that his red marks seemed to burn again. 'You'd take the word of a witch? They'll say anything to wriggle off the rope. I know these people. This one sent hell-fire to burn me . . . you were there, Holden . . . will you let the Devil get away with that?'

The magistrate frowned and chewed his lips. He had no wish to let that man get his hands on me or anyone else, but he believed in the Devil, and that I was a Devil's agent. Besides, he had his instructions from his masters in Lancaster – men who had given the Witch-hunter his powers. Perhaps Bawdwin was right. Perhaps torture was the only way.

'If God is to judge her, He will bring her to Him in His own way,' said Holden. 'I've known Isabel all her life. There's no harm in her unless it was put there by others and she has committed no crime. Unless scaring Witch-finder Bawdwin off his horse has been made a hanging offence.'

The Witch-finder leaned across the table and jabbed his words at the parson. 'Perhaps you are in league with them,' he hissed. 'You would not be the first witch to hide behind the Church's skirts.'

But now he had gone too far. Nowell snapped,

'Is that a formal accusation?'

The thin man shook his head reluctantly and sat down. 'She should hang,' he muttered. But the other two men ignored him, and turned to me.

'Speak, Issy,' said Holden. 'Tell us about Iohan a-Style.'

My tongue felt like clay. I confessed to being a witch myself. I confessed to throwing Bawdwin off his horse with the Devil's help. But I could not speak against Iohan.

Holden glanced at the magistrate. 'You know the danger you're in, Issy,' he said. 'Speak, in God's name.' I looked at him, and I could see his eyes pleading with me. But I could not speak.

'The Devil has her,' gloated Bawdwin. 'She cannot properly confess until it has been forced out of her.'

I saw Holden and Nowell glance anxiously at each other. Nowell leaned forward and tried once more. 'Isabel,' he said. 'You would be wise to tell us everything now. I have no wish . . .' He glanced at Bawdwin. 'I wish you would tell us everything now, Issy.'

His voice was urgent. He had seen Bawdwin at work. 'Please, Issy,' he repeated. I looked at him, at Holden, at the Witch-finder. I felt my soul chill inside me. But I could not betray Iohan.

Bawdwin sighed. 'She cannot,' he said

Parson Holden stood up. 'I want to speak to her alone for a moment,' he said. 'Perhaps I can convince her.'

'It'll do you no good,' said the Witch-finder. 'She is Satan's. You'll have to give her to me in the end.'

'Then she deserves every chance to avoid you,' replied the magistrate. He nodded at Holden and stood up. 'Listen to what the parson tells you, Isabel,' he told me. 'It would be happier for you to confess freely.'

He led the Witch-finder outside. The parson came round the table to sit next to me, as he had in Iohan's garden that sunny day. He mopped his face and smiled weakly.

'Here's a to-do,' he said. 'Some of the things I've seen in these past few days . . .' He shook his head again.

'You know she's a witch, don't you, Issy?' he asked me, and I nodded. 'Is that why you ran away?'

I told him how I followed her to the Sabbat and that I had seen the Devil there. He frowned.

'I wish you had left sooner.' He paused and chewed his lip. 'She's here, did you know that?'

'Iohan, here?'

'Oh, yes. There was an accusation – an old servant girl of hers – Joan.' He nodded his head towards the door and said in a bitter voice, 'She spent several hours in the company of our friend out there.'

It took a few moments to sink in. 'What did he do?' I asked. The parson shook his head. 'Is she alive?'

'She is, just. I don't know how. She's a brave woman, Issy, but no one could . . .' His voice trailed off. 'I'm sorry.'

'I want to see her,' I said, standing. 'You will let me see her, won't you?'

He shook his head. 'Not yet. You must confess first.'

I shook my head.

'She's confessed, Issy – everything. And she's accused you.'

'Me?'

'She told us everything. Who you are, what you've done. Don't blame her, Issy, she held out for a long time – too long. She wanted to give her friends time to get away. Don't you understand? In the end, everyone tells Bawdwin whatever he wants. You, too. She did everything she could.'

I nodded and sat back down. 'She told me that if they ever caught me I should tell them everything they wanted to know.'

'I wish she had followed her own advice. I was there. Bawdwin insisted . . . to witness the confession when it came.' He looked down at me. 'Issy, I want to spare you that. That man' – he nodded his head at the door again – 'he wants revenge for what you did to him. You have to tell, do you understand?'

I nodded my head. It was all at an end.

'You will confess?' he asked eagerly.

I nodded. 'Will she go to hell?' I asked.

He nodded. 'I don't believe she will,' I said

bitterly. 'She is a good person . . . just because she's not a Christian . . . just because she's different.'

Holden nodded. 'She was a witch, but she was good at heart. I hope God will be merciful to her, even though she worshipped a false god.' He spoke about her in the past, even though she was still alive – perhaps lying just a couple of metres away from me.

I had a sudden thought. She had told everything, the parson had heard. There was something I had to know. 'Did she tell you about the Sabbat?' I asked. I was remembering what Jennet had said. 'I have to know . . . was it . . . was it really the Devil I saw . . .'

The parson cleared his throat. 'She told us about the Sabbat,' he said. 'She doesn't call him the Devil. According to her it is an old god, a pagan god who has horns. She told us that it was the Christians who gave the Devil the old god's shape. But certainly it is the Devil. This god may visit them in their own minds, but it was not a real monster you saw, Issy. A man dresses up to represent him – usually a friend of hers, someone called Tolly, with a mask, I believe.'

Parson Holden bent and kissed my cheek before he went out to call for the magistrate to hear my confession.

Chapter 19

That night I awoke to the terror which was so familiar but always surprised me. The stillness of sleep exploded, violent light pounded and beat behind my eyes . . .

. . . the fire was before me, burning my face, my hands; the smell of my singed hair and clothes, the heat clutching my throat, stopping my breath, the choking smoke, the hard grip of the man who held me in the flames bruising my head and face. I'm fighting for breath, fighting to turn my head, fighting not to look – above all not to look. And then there was Iohan's voice . . .

'Look into the fire, Issy – look, look into the fire . . .'

She was still with me, even now. This time I believed her. I opened my eyes. I saw . . .

It was a woman's face that I had never dared remember – a face I knew and loved although I had denied her for so many years. It was a face very like my own. It was the still face of one who had finished her suffering. I felt happy as I dreamed, that she could not feel the fire or see me watching her. But the other me, the little girl that the soldier held aloft for the flames to lick knew no such thing.

Everything happened slowly, like a story, as the memory unfolded. The flames lapped at my mother, her clothes caught fire. There was my own terrifed scream: 'Don't hurt her . . . don't hurt my mummy!' Then there was the soldier shrieking as he twisted under my force and plunged into the flames, my own fall into the blazing embers. And then Iohan struggling for me in the fire, her hair ablaze, her bandaged hands pushing at the burning wood, the crowd jeering as she hauled me out across the embers and beat out the flames. I watched it all, remembering, listening to my own baby howls across the years.

I awoke shivering in the wet clay of the dungeon floor. Jennet was shaking me and stroking my face.

'There's no fire,' she whispered.

I shuddered and looked around me. Above me was a stroke of pale air from the window slit, letting in a whisper of night. Otherwise there was only the chilled darkness, the heavy, stinking air of the cell, and skinny, warm little Jennet pressing close to me.

'I wish there was a fire,' I whispered back. I squeezed Jennet tight, closed my eyes and I cried. Now I knew whose face I had seen in the fire and I understood why I had been so terrified. I could see her face clearly in my mind's eye now and forever and hear my own baby voice screaming for her over and over again . . .

We spent many more days down there. The thin

slit of light must have been hidden deep in the ground itself as it let in only the meanest light, casting pale shadows into our darkness. We woke, and fell asleep and woke again and there was no way of knowing whether an hour or a day or a week had passed. We spent most of our time huddled together on the damp mud in a corner, trying to keep warm. Sometimes we tried to climb up to sniff at the fresh air through the slit, because it stank down there – of cold clay, of stagnant water, of wet stone and above all of ourselves. The guard, who came once a day to feed us our slops, emptied the bucket only when it was overflowing.

At first we were expecting Parson Holden to come any day. Then we despaired of him ever coming; then we stopped waiting. Perhaps he and Nowell had failed to save us, perhaps Bawdwin had gone over their heads to the Justice in Lancaster again – or perhaps they were just keeping us to testify at the trials. We had no way of knowing and soon we stopped even caring. The mud dirtied us, the foul air soiled us, we became so much a part of the cell itself it seemed impossible to tell where the mud ended and we living creatures began. The fear disappeared behind boredom, the boredom behind hunger and at last a close, oppressive misery was all there was. Even dying seemed impossible in that place of no air; only misery could survive.

It must have been night when it happened as

there was no light when I awoke. There was a breeze blowing through the cell. At first I thought that a door far away in the prison had been opened to the night. Jennet too had awakened and she was sniffing at the air.

The wind increased. With the fresh air came wild scents. No prison stink here; this was the outdoors. It was the wind that blew over the woods at night, rich with wet leaves, grass, brambles, bark . . . I glanced at the door: locked. I glanced at the little slit above me: too miserable for such a big wind as this.

Jennet was crying. I could see her edging away, her little oval face white with fear. But I wasn't afraid; I was excited. There were leaves, real leaves blowing round the cell and brushing against our faces and our legs. I caught glimpses of the shadows of creatures flying past, galloping, chasing around the cell. The wind grew; leaves and twigs whipped around the walls and stung my skin, the wind roared and howled in my ears, emptying me, filling me up . . .

A hundred smells and visions rushed past; cattle in a frosty field, the smell of a fox, the call of a cat, the creak of a tree in the wind, ice cracking at the edges of a pond as some great beast came down at dawn to drink . . . warm breath, blood, tears, pain . . .

And then the moon came down. She rose through the stone into the dungeon with us, and every corner filled with silver light. The sense of living things all around us – burrowing, flying, calling, crying, growing – increased a hundred-fold. Jennet flung herself down in a heap in the corner and buried her face. Outside I heard the guards. They were running about like mice, shouting and screaming.

'The moon, the moon has come down!' I heard them crying. A face appeared briefly at the grid on our prison door, a white, terrified oval.

'Send the moon away, witch,' he begged me. But I had no power, I could only shake my head. Then the face vanished and I heard the man crashing about up the stairs.

Now the moon shone in the cell with me, clouds rushing past her face. And some great shape moved in front of the silver light.

He was too high and too broad for the tiny cell but it didn't matter. His shoulders rose up beyond the clenched fist of stone, his horns swept up into the night winds. His breath filled the air and his wide face looked down into mine. His eyes – above all his eyes – I was falling into those fierce blue eyes. They opened wider and wider, they were full of sky, they were as big as the world; they were the sky itself. High white clouds flashed past a blue sky, the wind roared and snatched at me and with a great gust blew me right off my feet. For a second I was rushed around the cell with the leaves in the wind and then I was dashed away, up from the dungeon and into the night sky. I was flying, riding the wind up so high I could brush the moon's cheek with my hand . . .

. . . we were rushing down, down through the clouds, down past the high crags, past the moors and the wooded valleys, right down to the earth. Through the woodlands and the pastures I flew, through the lanes and the hedgerows to the lakes, the great wide waters with the mist of the early morning on them and the swans' wings singing prayers as they flew past us to roost. I soared like a bird, I flapped my wings . . .

. . . I was the river, moving like a snake between my banks, sweeping over the earth and opening up over fields of sour mud into the sweet, salty sea. My life paused for a second, grew cool and green. Now I was the grass, the moss, the trees. I was the slow growing heart of plants, the life that breathed the sun and grew and never died . . .

Now the world beat red around me. It was the quick, red blood of beasts, the beat of their hearts, their sharp eyes, their fleet, hard life. I was racing over the grassland; I was a cat, a dog, a hare, I was swift and free and ready to die at any second. I ran for my life and for the joy of it, and at last I ran so fast that my feet left the ground and I spun out of that hot blood and up, up into the air and away back up to kiss the moon on the wings of a big, wild wind . . .

Then his eyes were above me, I fell again . . . and it was all over. Suddenly, I was back on the ground watching the clouds rushing past a blue sky with the wind in my hair.

*

It was just as Iohan had said. At that moment I stopped believing in the Devil and in evil. The Horned Man was the strength of life. It was neither good nor bad, it was the heartbeat of the world, of plants and creatures and earth and I was a part of it. I let that strength fill me up and overflow me, and fill the cell and the corridors and the whole building.

The wind dropped, quite suddenly. Leaves that had been rushing around the cell dropped to the ground, the scurryings and beatings that filled the air faded. The vision died. The smell of mud and filth returned, the moon vanished behind dark clouds that turned to stone. There was a lingering smell of the woods at night, I thought I heard a night bird call . . . and then I was myself again.

There was a noise in a corner and I saw Jennet. She was staring at me as she backed away up a pile of rubble in one corner. Her hand was on her face and she was shaking her head at me.

I held out my hand. 'Are you coming, Jennet?' I asked.

'Not with him . . . oh, no, not with him . . .' I went to the door and tried it. It was open. No doors would be closed against me on this night.

'Come with me,' I urged her. 'Do you want to go back to Malkin Tower? Come with me.'

Jennet shook her head. 'I'll pray for you,' she croaked. 'I won't tell,' she cried as I stepped outside into the dank corridor. I heard her call out to me one last time, 'I can't come . . . I don't dare come.' Then she scuffled down and I pulled the door closed behind me.

A few metres along was the other cell. I pushed the door open and went in.

She was a patch of dark in the darkness of her cell. They had manacled her so that she hung from the wall. I ran across and tried to embrace her, but she cried out. 'My hands, watch my hands,' she begged. Bawdwin had remembered his promise. I knelt by her and kissed her.

'I felt your dream,' she whispered. 'Now you are yourself again, despite everything they did.'

I nodded, but I couldn't speak. Even under her gown I could see how crooked her limbs were, how great dark patches spread across her cloak.

'In Scotland they burn the body of a witch after she is hanged . . . your mother felt no pain in the fire. She was my sister, Issy . . . so young. That soldier wanted you to see her burn . . . But now you're free to love her again.'

'We have to hurry . . .' I began.

'I have to stay,' said Iohan.

'But I can help you – you can lean on me. Please, you have to try.' I pulled at her, but she was too heavy. She cried out again and toppled back against the wall.

'I can't,' she panted, 'I'm finished, Issy . . .'

It was too late for her. Bawdwin had done his work well. 'Why didn't you tell them what they wanted?' I raged.

'I'm a stupid old woman, of course. But it gave some people a little time. Tolly got away. That's good, isn't it? It's my own fault . . . I couldn't give up the cloth,' she added. 'If I'd gone like Tolly said . . .'

I kissed her. Somehow I managed to hold her without hurting her.

'Tolly's gone south, down to Essex,' whispered Iohan. 'There are some of us left down there. You must try and find him. You must keep the memory of the Horned Man alive, Issy, because when we are all gone and he is forgotten, the world will begin to die.'

She kissed me. 'Now we say goodbye. Hurry up before the guards come.'

There was nothing I could do; she was too badly broken for any help. I kissed her once more and left her behind me. I found my way upstairs and into the clean night. It was late; there was no one about as I made my way past the close, grubby cottages. Soon the smell of the town with its smoke and its rubbish was behind me and I came to a finger of woodland running along a valley with a stream flowing like a shot of silver under the moon. The rich wet smells of the earth rose on the air around me. A night bird called, something rustled in the bracken on the sides of the valley and looking up, I saw the horned moon flying with the clouds next to heaven above me. I thought of Iohan in her filthy cell who would never see this night again and I sank down by the water and wept.

I felt I could never move again, that I had no more use for my life. But a few minutes later, some heavy bird or other creature flew into a tree above me. I looked up, and it called me. It was a strange call, that seemed to come from the throat of no bird or animal – a delighted, gurgling, laughing call that made me start with hope.

'Iohan!' I jumped up and cried out at the night. I waited and listened but the call was not repeated. Soon, something flew out of the branches; I heard dark wings carry it away. I knew that Iohan was free of her cell, her pain and her tormentors. I prayed for her. Then I pulled myself together and headed away south. I wanted to call on Nat and Ghyll before I made my way down to Essex, where I hoped to find Tolly and some other friends of mine.